I0662934

Blood Money
Tales from Two Continents

Scott Mastro

Savant Books and Publications
Honolulu, HI, USA
2012

Blood Money

Published in the USA by Savant Books and Publications
2630 Kapiolani Blvd #1601
Honolulu, HI 96826
http://www.savantbooksandpublications.com

Printed in the USA

Edited by Doris Chu and Daniel S. Janik
Back Cover Photo by Jackie Angle/Shutterpaws Photography
Cover Art and Design by Daniel S. Janik

13-digit ISBN: 978-0-9829987-5-5
10-digit ISNB: 0-9829987-5-9

Acknowledgement

Heartfelt thanks to Doris Chu and Daniel S. Janik for co-editing, and to my family and friends for encouragement and support.

When once the itch of literature comes over a man, nothing can cure it but the scratching of a pen. - Samuel Lover ~ *Handy Andy*, 1842

Chapter 1

The Desperate Breaths of Fallen Stars

In his mid-twenties and blessed with what life had brought him so far, the young Iranian glanced away from the similarly-aged Korean girl sitting across from him in front of the Parisian bistro's full-length window. They'd come here on their first date, halfway through the semester, enthused with the prospect of one another. Celebrating successful completion of final exams, neither knew the confession each was keeping from the other.

Against religious and parental wishes, he was beardless. Similarly, she was bare-legged, in sandals and shorts, their heresies fierce kindling in the fire of their mutual attraction. He renounced scripture and custom with his jeans and John Lennon t-shirt. She tempted the ancient gods with her bare arms and left-shoulder butterfly tattoo.

Their conversation ceased momentarily, but their thoughts did not. She was watching a waiter walk by. He was looking out the window. The warm, yellow, café light reflected their water-color silhouettes in the translucent window glass, embossing their wavering images on the evening sidewalk-world outside. Darkness ensuing, neither spoke the words that needed to be said, convinced they alone held the trump card that would decide their high-stakes game of love.

The young man stroked his black tresses gathered in a ponytail, the remainder flowing across his shoulders, making him look like a reincarnation of the Great Khan. Sipping his wine, he reflected on how he'd enjoyed this woman's company and how he'd accepted his impulsive feelings for her.

She glanced at him. Their eyes seized one another's.

She was petite, mysteriously Asian, skin the color of olive smoke, eyes green as sparkling emeralds, her laughter like a forest bird trilling for a creature of its own kind. Her smiles burst like a painter's zealous brush-strokes abandoning reality to revel in pure imagination.

His smile came with hesitation, a mouse watching for the raptor swooping to snatch this golden acorn in his possession. Moving his hand to his mouth, he thought it would hold his words in.

An ethereal shock-wave flashed through them simultaneously, for her, the epiphany of a new life heretofore hidden in their relationship, for him, a jolt of electric revelation.

She flipped her head reflexively, her hair tossing like an ocean swell undulating far from sight of land. Folding her delicate hands on the table and crossing her legs, she searched the words swirling in her head and for the right moment to say them. He noted the restaurant's chandelier-lights sparkling like stars above their heads in the window's reflection.

They'd come from their countries and cultures to study astronomy in Paris, sharing classes this past year, study sessions, long walks and this evening, the City of Light's spirit. Tonight would be a mystery in each one's heart to the end of their days.

She spoke no Arabic, he no Korean, their words never obstructing the universal language of the human body.

He motioned with his eyes, asking if she was ready to go. She hesitated, the continued tilt of her head suggesting regret with none of the exhilaration she'd indicated a moment before. Forcing a smile, she nodded reluctant agreement.

Slipping into summer jackets and reaching for one another's hand, they melded with the streaming flow of couples on evening promenade, a symphony of city-sounds encircling them. Navigating the busy intersection, what had been effortless earlier in the evening was now difficult on their leaving the bistro, him looking at his feet to match his longer stride to her shorter steps.

Walking towards the river Seine, he pointed at two ripe apples in a hotel-lobby window bowl. The fruit was like them, he said, then worried he'd misconveyed his intent, revealed too much. She slipped her arm through the crook of his and rested her head on his shoulder.

At the river, they turned along a foot-path that hugged the bank and stopped in the middle of a bridge to watch the water beneath them, suspended together in what Time could not touch.

She laid her head on his chest. He leaned his on hers. Anchored to one another, they watched the Seine course powerfully away from them, the midsummer-night sky offering their every unspoken wish, the universe pausing as one then a second solitary star flashed and fell to earth, each unable to join the other before striking the horizon.

Suspended in that eternal moment, their hearts sailed on moonbeams gone to light another world. Tears streaked the young woman's cheeks and she brushed them away, hoping he had not seen. Feeling her body move away from him like a paper boat loosed from a child's grasp, he sighed.

Arm-in-arm they walked to the end of the bridge, descending to the street and stopping beside a line of horse-drawn carriages. Looking into her eyes, he wrapped his arm around her waist and kissed her. She accepted, lifting onto her toes and closing her eyes. A nearby cab-man smiled. A car roared up the avenue, honked, and, tires squealing, disappeared into the darkness.

Kiss completed, they wended up the near-deserted boulevard, passing under a street lamp that had sputtered alive as if from the heat of their passion. She pointed at it, tracing an arc, indicating it was a fallen star returned. They laughed, he wanting to walk on the sidewalk, she in the street.

He needed to explain he was leaving for England, but was certain it would alter the evening. She needed to tell him she was emigrating to America and feared it would shatter their intersecting orbits. Walking, they tried to erase the distance their thoughts filled between them, the silence condemning their desire to the starlight of this evening only.

Their tale of two continents would take them to new worlds and other romances measured against this night, and their destinies would punish them with wonderment of how a life together might have been. The penance of their singular indiscretion was masked in kisses, caresses and tears falling like the desperate breaths of fallen stars. From the ashes of their untended fire, a fond ember of two misty-ghosted spirits in a restaurant window's reflection would haunt them forever, that last evening fraying to a single strand spanning their lives like the measure of the stars across the Milky Way.

Schooled as Parisian astronomers, their careers would become daily admonishments of the time they'd shared in the City of Light, and what had been lustful, tangible and youthful love-play, became a heavenly-cursed memory that would pursue them to the end of their days.

Chapter 2

Flutter and Drag

Looking out the second-story window of his grandmother's house in the Alhambra suburb of Los Angeles, six-year-old Roberto watched the birds drink and splash in the bird bath below, the window from which the summer before he'd tipped a shoebox full of baseball cards. The birds' hopping and flapping in the bird bath reminded him of the children scrambling to pluck the valuable cards out of the air as they fluttered to the ground, his only pleasant memory of the previous year.

Comic books replaced his baseball card obsession, and he plastered an entire wall of his room with their covers. Not sharing his enthusiasm for them displayed in such a disrespecful manner, his grandmother disgorged a litany of curses for defacing her wallpaper.

He ran away the next day, riding his bike until sundown, having no place else to go and wearing out his shoes from dragging his feet to stop his brakeless bike. Wondering if having a bike with no brakes made him poor, he knew it was why he was treated badly by family and strangers alike.

More puzzling was why his grandfather had died, denying his grandson the chance of knowing him. With no recollections of him, Roberto wondered if his grandfather's death was part of a larger family scheme to punish him for nothing he could think of he'd done.

Sometimes he thought his father was spying on him, to see if he was being good. Walking, he would look back to see if his father was behind him, or he'd run to the corner, duck around it and wait to catch a glimpse of his father following him. Riding in the car, he'd glance in store windows, hoping to spot his father watching as he went by, wondering why his father would play such a trick, maybe once as a joke, but not every single day. Now his grandfather had joined the game.

In his grandmother's house, he'd walk from room to room, inhaling each room's smells, hoping to breathe in something of his grandfather. The wood floors creaked beneath his feet.

His grandmother told him his grandfather would fall asleep in the overstuffed living room chair, the back of his head against the wall leaving an imprint in the plaster like Christ's face in the Shroud of Turin. Roberto believed the spot to be a place of sanctity, but he couldn't be certain if what she said was true. She read him the Bible. It told him to believe without question. Wanting to know something about his grandfather, he believed with blind faith. If he doubted her he'd have to doubt the Book, and he thought he knew where that would lead.

Sitting in his grandfather's chair, he would lay his head where his grandfather's had been, searching for memories. One day, his mind adrift, from another room his grandmother announced that she was going to church. Leaving, she snuck back and caught him with his head against the hallowed spot. Cackling and lashing a finger at his foolishness, she retrieved her Bible and waddled off to church, leaving him to wonder why the men in his family had abandoned him and the women enjoyed embarrassing him so.

Then an amazing thing happened. Walking in his grandfather's orchard, he saw green apples growing on red apple trees. Worrying that he, the only male survivor, might someday be challenged by the women in the family to recreate this miracle, he began a search for the secret of how his grandfather had accomplished this magic.

As a divorced man years later tracing his ancestral roots, he traveled to his grandfather's Mexican village and was told how, as a teenager, his grandfather had crossed the Rio Grande River and snuck into Texas, making his way to Los Angeles, never seeing his family and village again. The story made him wonder if his grandfather's leaving home and never returning had been as painful as it was for his grandson to live with his grandfather's wife. Roberto wanted to run away, too.

In the village church, he placed his hands in the marble font his grandfather had been baptized in and imagined a pink baby crying as the holy water splashed its forehead. In the church cemetery, Roberto knelt and wept for his grandfather and the family he never knew. In the village orchard, he saw green apples on red apple trees and relived the childhood magic.

The world had proven different from how he'd imagined as a child it would one day be. Concern for each day and fear for the future among the people working his ancestral lands were mirrored in the faces of those in his country. As a boy, he'd believed people would one day live in harmony. As an old man, he saw a world robbed of its magic. Someday there would be no more green apples on red apple trees. His own children had grown up disheartened, disinterested.

In Alhambra, he took his grandchildren to see his grandparents' house. The bird bath was there, but the orchard was overgrown, the trees skeletal remains of what they had once been. Walking to the top of the hill, he told them a story about baseball cards fluttering in the air like sparrows and a boy dragging his feet until his shoes were worn through. Hugging them to him, he recited a tale of two boys hurling down this very hill on one bike, the boy in front dragging his feet, the boy in back whooping in delight while fingering the baseball cards in his pocket. Roberto pointed to where the bike careened into the intersection and a car slammed into them full-speed, the cards in the hand of the boy on the back exploding into the air like sparrows flapping in a bird bath, fluttering unclaimed to the ground. He pointed in the direction from which the ambulance came, lights flashing, siren wailing, taking the boys away. When the ambulance had gone the children in the crowd rushed on hands and knees to retrieve as many cards as they could.

That was the end of the story, but as they walked down the hill, he remembered something else. That day, a boy their age looked at the baseball cards scattered on the ground and no longer had any desire to collect them. That day he learned how things lost their magic, and it didn't matter whether anyone wanted it to come back, it would never return. He wondered what tragedies his grandchildren would have to endure before they learned that lesson for themselves.

Chapter 3

Getting Into Heaven With Little or Nothing Down

Everyone in the Italian village some kilometers east-northeast of Rome knew that, except for public and religious holidays, no matter what the weather, the same *giardiniere* (gee-*ar*-dee-nee*air*-ray = *gardener*) would be sitting in front of the village welcome center well before it opened, and today was no exception. Dressed in a light-plaid shirt, pleatless dark-green trousers, grey tweed jacket and matching cabby hat, his black, round-toed, lace-up work boots completed the outfit that in part made him and the welcome center an international tourist stop. The *giardiniere* appeared every morning like the long hand of a clock that couldn't wait for the starting hour to begin, accurately anticipating the moment a welcome-center clerk would grip the door-handle, open the building and usher everyone in. Having long ago surrendered to the drudgeries of repetitive daily tasks, the clerk arrived at work like a clock that could have waited another thirty minutes for the work day to begin.

The village population was evenly divided on God's track record, half praising His work as top-notch, half declaring it a shoddy affair so far. Similarly, half of the welcome center staff thought it sheer bedevilment how the human icon sitting in front of their center every forenoon could be so consistently dedicated to something as speculative as the Lord's will, but there he was, Bible in one hand, religious baubles in the other.

The welcome center opened at ten precisely. Prepared to earn his daily bread, on cue, the *giardiniere* stood, sensing the Lord's descent from Heaven reanimating his mortal coil, and like the Pope running late for his coronation, presented identification at the information desk then bee-lined to the community room where, out-of-sight, the *Gesù* (*Jay*-soo = Jesus) peddler prepared for the hippy-type transcontinental trekkers who would soon be genuflecting their dollars before him. Preaching the gospel according to himself, *gratis* (grah-tee—for free), always with the thought of doing a little business after the sermon was completed, it was common knowledge to just about everyone except the welcome center staff, even listed in several English-language travel guides, that the *giardiniere's* currency was eighth and quarter ounce marijuana denominations hidden in the hollow interior of the Bible that never left his grasp.

From the more naïve, he accepted nominal fees for candles, vials of holy water and other papal paraphernalia obtained, he assured the purchaser, from sources close to the Papacy, for it was well-known in the backstreets of the Vatican that he traded for these trinkets with the marijuana grown between his hillside grape–rows, and bottles of a varietal wine produced solely on his farm. When not in attendance at the welcome center, he mingled with priests and administrators seeking to exchange coveted religious curios for his secular offerings, these transactions justified by church officials and underlings with the maxim that one must sin in order to be saved.

Many a Vaticanicater swore on his mother's life and the blessed blood of the Virgin Mary that a single bottle of his DOCG, the name for his un-classified, regional vintage, shortened by unofficial papal decree to "dog," and a lungful of his spirited cannabis could get the nuns dancing out of their habits every time, the aroma of his Super Tuscan infusing a papal chamber like incense at High Mass, inviting mind and body to gambol and frolic with Bob Marley's ghost.

The *giardiniere's* audience today was a solitary, frizzy-haired *giovane* (gee-oh-*vawn*-ay = young man) in sandals, bib-overalls and wire-rimmed glasses, the one exception to his classic backpacker image being a black briefcase. The *giovane* stepped forward and offered a courteous, "*Dov'è il bagno?*" (*Doh*-vay il *ban*-yo = Where is the bathroom?) to which the *giardiniere* pointed down the hall.Clutching his briefcase to his chest like a soccer ball signed by AS Roma's Francisco Toti, the *giovane* nodded, laid his attache on the table and excused himself. Giving the hallway a summary glance, the *giardinere* retreated backwards into the conference room.

Some afternoons on the village piazza (pee-*ats*-uh = square), a man looking and dressing like Jesus appeared on a unicycle, clutching at the air to pluck sinners from it. Balanced as if God was on one shoulder and the Devil on the other, One-Wheeled Jesus mesmerized the crowd as the *giardiniere's* opening act, the two men smiling like Cheshire cats, one filled with the Lord, the other, dog and weed.

The *giardiniere* would sit silent, head bowed like Mary awaiting the angel Gabriel to come tell her she was with Child while the unicyclist eyed awed on-lookers, verifying they were tourists and not undercover police. Watching his warm-up act, the *giardiniere* imagined

Mary struck dumb by the prospect of telling her husband how she'd become pregnant without his assistance.

This morning, like every other at five minutes to ten, the *giardiniere* witnessed the miracle of a highly-polished, Egyptian-blue "Mother F" Farrari roaring up and screeching to a stop before the information center. All eyes scrutinized the woman-driver resembling Sophia Loren at the height of her movie career alighting from the car, tugging the hem of her skirt, popping the vehicle's boot and extracting a weather-worn Bible matching the *giardiniere's*. Dazzled by her titillating appearance, like the Virgin Mary's image in the wooden-slat siding of a chicken coop or the rings of a tree stump, no one noticed her sleight-of-hand, exchanging the one on his lap for the one in her hand, the switch performed so adeptly the *giardiniere* believed he'd been touched by the Lord and the Devil simultaneously. Eyelashes fluttering like doves taking wing from Vatican Square, she flashed the crowd a card-game smile, climbed into the Mother F and screeched away, leaving an unholy cloud of dust where the sleek sports car had been.

As effortlessly as Nosferatu whisking across an open field at midnight, the *giardiniere* sequestered himself in the conference room, sitting at its massive dark-wood table, making the sign of the cross and eyeing the briefcase. From a small, round, stained-glass window high up on the exterior wall, the sun's kaleidoscopic rays showered him in a rainbow of pastel light. Illuminated thusly, he whispered, "Give us our daily bread," laid his Bible on the table and popped the briefcase's latches. Inside was a Holy Trinity of three twenty dollar bills, a foot-and-a-half long glass bong and a bottle of Pepto-Bismol. Having never seen Pepto-Bismol, he could only guess the pink liquid's mind-altering characteristics. Wanting to smell and taste its intriguing composition, but fearing time was against him, he latched the briefcase's lid, knowing what U.S. dollars and the glass tube were for.

The young American entered the room and joined the *giardiniere* at the table. After perfunctory words of God, the *giardiniere* pushed his Bible to the middle of the table, cueing the Euro-traveler with his eyes. The American opened it, transferred the plastic bags to his briefcase, replaced them with the twenties, closed the briefcase and pushed the Bible to the Italian. The light from the stained glass window intensified.

Over the years, the *giardiniere* had learned to never allow more than three people in the conference room at one time, the number he and God could maintain full attention on during such 'denominational' dealings, not wanting to call staff attention to an iordinate influx of convertees to the Catholic faith, imagining how unnerving it would be to arrive at the entrance to *Paradiso* (Pair-uh-*dee*-so = Heaven) and find a crowd milling as Saint Peter checked references, accepting a perk or payola from those whose records were less than irrefutable. One day he'd be among them, bartering for his soul. One day, but not today.

Homily and Eucharest satisfactorily consummated, the *giardiniere* steered the young traveler to the *ingresso* (een-*greh*-so = foyer). Clutching his briefcase as if it now housed his *vivo* (*vee*-voh = soul), the *giovane* whispered, "God's blessing to you," travel guide code-words indicating buyer gratification. Genuflecting to the American, the *giardiniere* reflected on how pleased Little Miss Mother F would be when they made their afternoon rendezvous at the corner café.

Pondering his upcoming Vatican visit, Bible in hand, satchel of sacred curios over his shoulder like a poacher with a poked pig, he stepped from the cobblestone curb into the path of a transcontinental tour bus, several of its passengers having made the journey to purchase his internationally-infamous wares.

Brakes screeching, dust billowing, his bundle of papal paraphernalia took wing like the spirit of a recently-deceased-and-paid-in-full parishioner rushing to get a seat at the right hand of the Lord, the twenties disbursing aerodynamically as if delivered from God's own automated teller machine.

Hobbling towards the proverbial light-at-the-end-of-the-tunnel, the impact had catapulted his shoes from his feet. His last earthly thought being, *no shoes, no shirt, no service*, he made instant inventory of his shirt and jacket, wondering if his entrance into Eternity would be hindered by crossing into the Hereafter in stockinged feet. Awaiting Heaven's glorious and all-forgiving love to swaddle him like a mangered baby, he hadn't registered any tangible sign that the Eternity he'd told himself and so many others about embodied a shred of truth in its carcass, but a more needling issue was pricking him.

Approaching a bottle-neck of smoky souls, the line into Heaven had slowed. Uncertain if his earthly actions would be sufficient to red-carpet him through Saint Peter's Gate, he rummaged his pockets for some inducement, relieved to find an orphaned nugget of Tuscan Super the Vatican crowd was all 'wow' about.

Chapter 4

Fishing Day

In the years since he'd held a stick with a bit of line and makeshift hook in his Huckleberry Finn hands, Mahalo (Mah-*huh*-low = thank you) had abandoned his Hawaiian-Big Island country-roots to embrace city life in the town of Hilo (*Hee*-low). Unlike his fellow workers whose bodies had grown rounder and whose minds had curved in on themselves, Mahalo had maintained his physical and mental vitality, and, for a man in his late forties, his youthful vigor was apparent in his full head of black hair, smooth, swarthy skin and well-defined facial features; a masculine jaw and prominent cheekbones were unencumbered by the lackadaisical effects of television on his brain and fast food on his midsection.

With spring's affirmation of better things to come, Mahalo took up the odd *haole* (*Haw*-lee = non native Hawaiian) sport of fly-fishing, first, to satisfy his dog, Hula's (*Hoo*-luh = dance), curiosity for the sport and second to supply them a fresh, healthy meal. Assuming Hula's primal fascination with fishing was spurred by the wildly staring eyes and gasping mouths flip-flopping on shore, he purchased the necessary pole, hooks, flies and, begrudgingly, the mandatory fishing license, patriotically ahdering to the credo that fishing was an inclination inherent in the Constitution and should not be bureaucratically-monitored in any manner whatsoever.

Assuring Hula that seafood *was* on this evening's menu, they assumed coordinated positions beside a local creek bounded by massive granite boulders on the near side and jagged rock outcroppings on the opposite bank, Mahalo fancying his line flaring out over the leaping rapids and swirling eddies to moments later haul in the proverbial fish–that-swallowed-Jonah. Interpreting Hula's sniffing the air and pawing the dirt as a call to action, he commanded her to follow him up the trail leading away from the last vestiges of civilization, pondering the difference between a brook, creek and stream as they went, while explaining to a dumb-founded Hula it had to do with where one was from.

Flora and fast-moving water kneaded the minutes until time gave way to the simple succession of their muted footsteps. Pole slung tip-back over his shoulder, his canine bounding up the rocks, Mahalo whistled a tune he thought common to simple country folk, morphing the whale he'd envisioned minutes earlier into pan-sized fish he would soon be reeling in. To his and Hula's delight, the pole quivered and jerked in response to his daydreaming.

Jarred from this reverie, he received his first lesson in fly-fishing. Despite his self-confidence, he'd managed, with no effort on his part whatsoever, to entangle a considerable length of fishing line in the branches they'd passed along the trail.

His initial reaction was to aggressively reel in the translucent line strung out like an errant Christmas garland on the red and green *ti* (tee = a native plant) bushes. Instead, he lowered and extended the rod in the direction of the tangle, mindful not to entwine the pole, methodically retrieving as much as he could like a mild-mannered Buddha within the confined space of the overgrown foliage. A minute of that and the realization he was losing ground *and* patience, he issued a caveman grunt, wrenched the pole upwards and, jerking the line taut, admonished the bushes to release what was, by purchase and taxation, legally his. Being of an entirely different species and social strata, the bushes ignored him. Hula however did not.

Recognizing the searing tone of the savage

vindictives flying above her, she tried to assess to whom or what if not her they were directed. Acknowledging her unease, Mahalo assured Hula his outburst was in no way meant for her and resumed relaxing the line and reeling it in, coming to the very Zen conclusion that, like some women he'd known, as easily as a line went out, it was unlikely to return as succinctly.

When the monofilament had given all the slack it could, he laid the rod on the moist, red-brown trail and rationally approached the problem of the remaining length. Taking up the pole, he called Hula to accompany him the way they'd come, reclaiming more of the line as they went. Glancing in the direction they'd been going and glad to be in her master's good graces again, Hula turned and followed, displaying interest in the elusive string her master was now literally wrapping himself in. Thinking it a game she too might find fun in, Hula leaped towards him and Mahalo unleashed another volley of curses, her master's finger having been gouged by the hook flying in opposite but equal reaction to his dog's excited tug. Unaware he had hooked his first catch of the day, she assumed whatever he was angry about must be directly related to something she had done, so she cowered and backed away.

He removed the intrusive barb from his hand while

reassuring Hula that the trouble was not of her doing. Instinct told her she should observe him from a distance. Winding the remaining disentangled line into the reel, he called for her to continue in the direction they had been going.

Spirits renewed, they headed upstream again, Mahalo in the lead, Hula dutifully-but-cautiously matching the lively pace dictated by her master. As he walked, he searched the water for a wide, calm area. The creek, however, neither slowed nor widened. Instead it narrowed and steepened, presenting even fewer places from which to level a rod and release its line. The situation led him to conclude, all the good fishing was downstream where they'd begun.

When he reversed course and commanded his dog to follow, Hula hesitated, thinking that the point was to get *out* of town. Nonetheless, as Mahalo started downhill, Hula ran to catch up, her canine brain concluding her master's determined pace in the opposite direction meant he knew where even more adventure awaited.

Keeping to the main trail to avoid a mishap like the one on the way upstream, they surprised a family of *Nene* (*Neh*-neh = Hawaiian geese) waddling at the water's edge. Without warning, Hula sprang in barking pursuit. The adult geese honked alarms and turned on webbed heels, keeping themselves between the threatening beast and their gaggle of goslings. Shooing their offspring towards the shore-weeds, geese and goslings leaned into their fleeing like racehorses running neck-and-neck to the finish line.

Knowing Hula to be more for the chase than the confrontation, Mahalo dropped his pole and raced to keep her from getting pummeled by the outraged birds. His concerns actualized when the goslings disappeared into the rushes and the adult geese, assured of their progeny's safety, turned and ground to a determined halt, establishing a defensive skirmish-line.

Too far behind to shoo the adult geese away, Mahalo watched as the feathered parents squared on the charging canine and, hissing like snakes, at the last possible moment dodged to either side, causing their antagonist to overshoot them. Teaching this domesticated creature the follies of treating a life-and-death experience like a backyard, suburban game, the female nipped Hula's nose as the dog flew past. Helpless to halt her forward momentum, Hula slid on the wet grass by the side of the stream. Leaving their four-legged nemesis on her belly with legs splayed in each cardinal direction, the adult *Nene* geese ruffled their wings and waddled into the underbrush, encouraging their goslings to join them.

Running to soothe Hula's injury and embarrassment, Mahalo slipped, overshot her *and* the bank and slid torso-first into the mud and water. Mission complete, the geese steered their brood away from the ghastly apparitions splayed half on shore, half in the stream.

Crouching in submission, Hula dragged herself to the bank where her master was hauling himself out of the creek, shirt and pants drenched. Peering up at him, she glanced sideways, her way of saying, "This is all my fault, isn't it?"

Mahalo's anger and frustration for his own plight crumbled when he saw his sweet-natured Hula licking a trickle of blood from her nose, and whether faked for the sake of gaining his sympathy or not, limping on her right, rear leg. As he crouched, hands outstretched to meet her approach, Hula rolled onto her back and submitted her underbelly in surrender.

Beginning with the bridge of her snout, he massaged her all over, examining her to make certain she had not been injured. Moistening a thumb, he daubed her nostril, removing the remaining blood, then scratched behind her ears, reflecting on how simple an act as fishing could have such unforeseen consequences. A minute passed, then another. Mahalo stood and told Hula to come along. Glancing in the direction of her tormenters, she shook herself and put some hop in her step to catch up.

In Hilo, man and beast considered their options. There were several locations where a fisherman might come to full terms with his quarry, imagining the thrill of standing on the bridge and imparting majestic casts upstream, but signs that looked like they'd been hand-painted by Hawaiian Homeland Security posted at both ends of the structure offered a hefty fine and/or lengthy imprisonment to anyone partaking in such terroristic activity.

Aware they'd walked the entire length of stream and ruminating on his piscine plan, Mahalo came to a decision. Visualizing succulent fish sizzling in a pan, he approached the bank, knowing what he must do, and bounded onto a rock several feet from shore, announcing to himself, Hula and the water, "This is the place."

Clutching the pole as if preparing for a sword-fight and determined to regain his dog's respect, Mahalo checked his footing and prepared to cast. Sensing this might be a spot they'd be staying in awhile, Hula curled about his feet, her aching nose pointed protectively towards the water. Swinging the tip adroitly behind him, he brought the pole up, around and forward, the line cracking like a whip on its way to a sweet spot where fish were waiting hungrily, but instead of the expected swish of the fly in the desired direction, he heard a yelp at his feet as Hula leaped from her prone position the same moment he felt a solid tug in the fly-rod's grip. Despite his desire to haul in a prize lunker, he knew it wasn't to be. Hula bounded into the stream, howling with pain, the hook embedded firmly in her rump.

Abandoning the pole, Mahalo splashed into the water, scooped up his struggling girl and thrust her onto the rock, pulling himself out after her. Wincing with pain, Hula was again lost as to what she had done to be thrice maligned, and searched for a sign that would help her understand what she needed to stop doing to cause her master such displeasure.

Secured with one of his hands, Hula yelped as Mahalo freed the barb from her tender flesh with a quick jerk. Consoled, she laid at his feet again as Mahalo wound up and cast a second time.

At the backward snap, Hula flinched. The line rippled forward in an elegant arc. As the fly touched the water, Mahalo began taking up the slack. Unable to do it fast enough, Mahalo watched the line pass downstream, under the bridge, over a waterfall, and snag in a stream-side bush. Disappointed but not discouraged, Mahalo lumbered ashore, Hula following despite his encouragements for her to remain on the rock, the day having proven too precarious to let her master out of her sight.

Maneuvering to where the fly was, he loosed the hook, while Hula sat faithfully on the bank, watching.

Mounting their creek-side citadel once more, Mahalo cast downstream, avoiding the falls, instead entangling hook and line in a patch of overhanging briars on the far side. Engrossed in his fly rescue-endeavor, Mahalo heard the *Hawai'i Pono 'i* (Ha-*vah*-ee *Po*-no *ee* = the Hawaiian state song), and saw the singing Department of Land and Natural Resources officer approach.

Verifying the status of Mahalo's soaked fishing license and warning of the penalties for fishing from the bridge, the warden added insult to injury by issuing a dog-off-leash citation. Securing Hula, Mahalo returned to his rock. The fish and wildlife ranger approached again, this time issuing a ticket for fishing within fifty feet of a public causeway, inquiring if Mahalo had any further questions. The fisherman asked if the officer knew who'd written the *national* anthem, how many Amendments there were to the Constitution and what six times nine equalled, leaving the conservation official to meditate on whether his lacking elemental knowledge of the greater nation as well as simple mathematics gave him authority under God and Man to enforce state and local statutes.

Away from the warden's prying eyes, Mahalo studied the infractions, rehearsing his courtroom soliloquy of how stupid most *haole* laws were. Not seeing Hula and thinking she'd strayed, he called for her in a loud voice, to find her regarding him attentively from behind. Apologizing for this grievous insult to her faithful canine personage, he regained her flagging confidence with well-meant caresses and earnest words of assurance.

Determined to make something of the unyielding day, he cast upstream, away from the bridge he had recently purchased, and whether it was over-zealousness or a misfire of brain synapses, the rod *and* reel flew from his hand, arching out over the rolling whitewater to exactly where he'd willed only the fly and line to go. Witnessing the pole bobbing away from him downstream, Mahalo leaped ashore in pursuit, and headed for the falls beneath the bridge. Responding to her master's order to follow, Hula wondered how this new adventure would end, secured as she was to her master and their mutual fate.

Running along the shore and monitoring the pole's aquatic advancements, Mahalo asked himself how much time and effort he was willing to commit to preserving his investment in what now seemed an exercise in futility. Thinking it possibly best to accept his losses and take up bicycling or tennis instead, he vowed to keep his fishing misadventure between himself and Hula as he watched the pole flip and tumble over the falls.

Clearing the churning froth, it bobbed to the surface on his side of the stream, taunting him to rescue it, to which he acquiesced. Crouching on the bank, he calculated he could lean out and snag the pole with the aid of a dead branch, but, when he tried, his footing failed and, arms thrashing, he crashed into the water, pulling Hula in, too.

As if sensing pursuit, the pole moved further downstream to where the *nene* they'd battled were observing Mahalo's unnatural human behavior with typical wild goose disdain. Hauling himself and Hula out of the creek, Mahalo swore to continue his mission on *terra firma*. Several times over the next half hour he thought he could make contact with the pole, but, more cautious now, each attempt failed.

Tracking it to where the water's force corralled the pole close enough so that, lying on his stomach, he could grasp it, he was at last rewarded with success. Lifting and shaking it triumphantly like the head of a defeated adversary, the line was playing out of the reel away from him. Thinking it snagged in dozens of places, he began reeling it in. Feeling a sudden tug strong enough to pull the tip of the rod down into the water, he realized that in spite of his efforts to the contrary, a fish had nonetheless become securely hooked.

To Hula's barking encouragement, Mahalo reeled the monster in and dragged the beast ashore. In her frenzy, leaping at it and taking the fish's head in her mouth and shaking it, she cried out, having embedded the hook in her jowl.

Confining a struggling Hula between his legs, Mahalo removed the hook with one hand while keeping the flopping fish from escaping with the other. Curiosity sated, Hula sat licking the inside of her cheek, trying to fathom why her master would try to choke the life out of her.

Walking home, fish dinner in her master's hand, she eyed the scaly sea creature with guarded interest, nudging it with her nose, careful not to give her master or it any reason to harm her again. Running ahead and sniffing in the tall grass, she found a tennis ball and brought it to him. Mahalo, taking it as a hint that he was better suited to playing fetch than fishing, to quash the notion, tossed the ball as far as he could. Shooting into the forest, Hula retrieved it, set it at his feet, and instantly forgave him the tribulations he'd set upon her earlier in the day. Surviving his trial-by-water and fish-in-hand to prove his acumen, Mahalo felt like a full initiate in the glorious and clandestine order of seasoned *haole* fly-fishermen, taking his place beside Captain Ahab and Huckleberry Finn in the historic analogues of great Americans who'd set out to find a fish and reel it in.

As the sun receded behind the hills, man and dog headed home, Hula muzzling *her* catch, dividing her interest between the ball and soon-to-be fish dinner, while Mahalo proudly displayed his victory against nature to every passerby that cared to see.

Chapter 5

Mr. Emm's Bucket

One particularly memorable Friday morning, a bleary-eyed, blood-shot sun dragged itself over the nagging Camden Town horizon of London's metropolis and spread its concentrated, lemon-curd warmth on the personage of Mr. Emm, a middle-aged, mid-level advertising manager at the firm of Chilbains and Doolap. Plopping into the bright yellow breakfast nook of his compact, suburban brownstone, he was contemplating his regularly-scheduled tea and muffins in his, as the French would say, normally *bien existence*.

Having awakened in his usual manner at his usual time, he rolled back the sheets and like a good *homo sapiens*, sat upright…to find a bucket where his head should be. As to the *who, what, when* and *why* of how it came to be there, he was at a loss, but as to its *where*, he could, with the solid determination of a seasoned cartographer, say it was *on* his head. Being of a normally cheery disposition, he noted that the bucket was snug, but not uncomfortably so and summed the situation thusly: "If a bloke's got to go around with a bucket on his head, it should bloody-well fit like a glove."

Donning slippers and robe, he shuffled to the bathroom and gazed mirror-ward, thinking to wrestle his usual shock of unruly hair into submission, but all he got for his efforts was a ringing thud, reaffirming that a washer-man's accoutrement was indeed occupying him *á la tête*. Bracing himself to the sink like a ballerina against her *barre*, he lathered and razored his chin, wondering if his hair-trim scheduled for later in the week would better serve him if canceled. Satisfied with what of his ablutions he could complete, Mr. Emm folded his towel squarely, hung it on its rack and scuffled to his wardrobe.

In the hallway, his wife shrieked.

"It's a bloody bucket, is all," he told her as calmly as if he was wearing a bowler hat.

Despite his apparent lack of concern, Mrs. Emm, thinking as hard as she might, could come to no explanation as to why the man she'd shared her life with for fifteen years should end up with his head in such a device and was paralyzed with fear of how his present condition might affect his role as the family's sole bread-winner in these dangerously troubled times, mortgage payments, utility bills and their daughter's upcoming university tuition, to name her most prevailing financial preoccupations.

Eavesdropping on her parent's conversation, charming Zoonie, the sole and blessed culmination of their marriage, heard the words "bucket" and "head" yet no portion of her teenage mind allowed the notion that those two words related in any way to her father's physical person let alone in tandem, or more correctly, in vertical and adjoining relation to his head. Had she even an inkling of what awaited her at the breakfast table that morning, she would have crawled under her covers to sleep a thousand days. Then again, having an interest in theater, in particular, Japanese *Kabuki,* she might have gladly fallen upon an authentic *tonto* knife in ritual, samurai-like suicide. Unfortunately, there wasn't one in the house.

Concluding it might be some youthful prank spawned in her husband's university days, Mrs. Emm tried to associate today's date with a corresponding fraternal ceremony, but Mr. Emm shunned the notion.

"Nothing of the sort," he said, nicking his bucket on the corner of the bedroom door-molding as he skirted his wife and her preposterous allegation. Feeling his way to the dressing closet, he fitted himself with argyles, garters, crisp suit pants, white shirt, suit-vest, a red tie with thin gray horizontal lines, gold tie-clasp and black, mirror-shined shoes. Suit jacket over his arm, he made his way downstairs, relying on the railing more than usual, pledging to maintain his pluck and make the most of the day despite this unexplainable encumbrance. As if any meal with her parents let alone one where her father insisted on wearing a bucket on his head throughout was a form of evil, Chinese torture, Zoonie rolled her eyes and slurped her cereal.

"A young lady doesn't slurp her cereal," her mother reminded. Zoonie slurped louder, hurling dagger-eyes at her father, the living, breathing embodiment of proof her parents were out to make her the most mocked adolescent in British history.

"Look at that, will you, dear?" Mr. Emm said, squinching his eyes and contorting his neck muscles to peek out from under the bucket's rim at the kitchen television. "The American Vice President's former corporation is in litigation in their Supreme Court and the Vice President and the judge hearing the case have gone duck-hunting. That's American justice for you," adding, "and it confirms the value of doing one's business from an undisclosed location." Zoonie wished someone would confine *her father* to an undisclosed location.

Thinking her husband ought to be more concerned with his own predicament than "foul" play and the American Vice President, Mrs. Emm summed her sentiments thusly: "Another muffin, dear?"

"No, just the same, I've got to get on to work." Mr. Emm stood and, meaning to dab his mouth with his napkin, ran it across the bucket's embossed brand name, Plungent Technologies. "We're finalizing a big account today and I've got to be in top form." Shoving his chair flush with the table, he tipped two fingers in salute from the 'P' of the red, blue, and silver label. Bending to kiss his wife made for an awkward moment, but not so nearly as when he attempted the same with his daughter.

"Ow," Zoonie said, wincing, throwing her hands up and thrusting her head to the side like a boxer parrying a punch.

"You get off to school right now, young lady, or you'll be late," her mother scolded. Zoonie couldn't see Mr. Emm's paternal smile, hearing only, "Study hard."

"Study hard and don't have a bucket on your head," she said, grabbing her coat, hat and satchel and skittering out the door.

"Perhaps we should call the plumber who fixed the washer hose?" Mrs. Emm ended her question with sufficient tonal up-swing to leave the final decision to her husband.

"It's a bucket, not a washer hose. This is a mistake of some sort I'll have worked out before your luncheon at the Ladies' League," Mr. Emm promised, framing his cranial incapacitation in terms of a parcel mis-delivered to him instead of his neighbor, Mr. Pimm, or a Mr. Emm in some other section of the city.

"I'll fix something nice for dinner," Mrs. Emm said, clearing the breakfast dishes, hoping that her reference to a wholesome evening's respite would make a noticeable difference in their increasingly uncertain world. "Will you be okay then?"

"It's a bucket, not another Middle East conflict," Mr. Emm said, emphasizing his positiveness with a wink no one on earth could have possibly seen. Feeling for the doorknob, he made his way down the front steps, using the handrail and descending carefully to the curb, counting the steps as he went, "One, two, three, four, five."

Walking the several blocks to the Underground, away from his wife's strained gaze and his daughter's pained emulations, Mr. Emm allowed himself to introspect upon his perplexing predicament. Habituated to popping off Beatle songs when a bit of whimsy was called for or as now, to lessen the grip of strained reflection, he swung into *Maxwell's Silver Hammer* until he realized the fatal phrase of hammers coming down on heads left him with the dreadful thought of a silver hammer crashing his bucket, causing irreparable damage to its contents. He might have lingered longer in this wicked day-mare if it hadn't been for a dog barking at his feet, the mutt's yapping bringing Mr. Emm to his senses.

"Scat!" he commanded. Startled by the roar booming from inside the bucket, the dog moved away.

Descending into Camden Town Station, Mr. Emm felt like Jacques Cousteau entering an underwater cave, but to his good fortune, the bucket gave him the canine-like ability to hear his train approaching a good ten seconds before anyone else, allowing him, with deep-sea diver precision, to maneuver to the lip of the platform before the other commuters, thus garnering a double-seat to himself.

Claiming the extra personal space like a poker player gathering his winnings, he was beginning to believe his luck was changing and this head-nonsense would soon turn in his absolute favor. Digging into the Liverpool lads' musical treasure trove, he imagined himself *carrying a weight, carrying a weight a long time*, but the suggestion put a kink in his *esprit* so he shifted his thoughts to a tune that left him admitting things were *getting better all the time.* Oblivious to the gawks and glares of his fellow commuters, he finalized his new confidence by elongating the syllables *get-ting-so-much-bet-ter-all the-time.* Screeching into Victoria Station, the train spat its riders from their climate-controlled cocoon into London's grey light, Mr. Emm thinking as he exited that, across town, his darling Zoonie would at this moment be settling into her homeroom meditation.

In fact, she was. Checking that she had everything she'd need for today's lessons, Zoonie was interrupted by a classmate's unwanted query. "Was that your father wandering the Underground with a bucket on his head this morning on the telly?" Zoonie looked about for an undisclosed location *she* could confine *herself* to.

At the firm of Chilblains and Doolap, news of Mr. Emm's bucket spread from receptionist Regina's desk, its shock-waves moving with tidal velocity from her front-and-central location like a tsunami itching to smack land. Fending an initial barrage of queries, Mr. Emm was then free to adroitly focus every fiber of his mid-level managerial being on preparing for his all-important afternoon presentation. Performing one hundred percent would translate to a well-deserved and long-anticipated promotion, yielding top-notch collegiate options for Zoonie, who was presently considering a career as a *ninja* assassin, beginning with killing the next person to participate in the apparently worldwide plot to get her laughed out of Saint Helena's Academy for Girls.

Co-workers' curiosities quelled, Mr. Emm arranged his morning to be bereft of commands, requests and conversations save one compliment from Jason, the office boy. Wheeling his postal cart with all the youthful pluck necessary to banish life's indenturing foibles, Jason proclaimed, "It's a *very* nice bucket, sir."

Lunch-time came in like Oscar Wilde and went out like Gilbert and Sullivan, Mr. Emm serenading his noon meal with the Fab Four's *Ob-la-di, Ob-la-da,* recounting how one Desmond had a marketplace barrow and that said love-interest, Molly, was a singer in a band. Desmond's *ob-la-dees, ob-la-das* sent the young man to a jeweler's for a ring and, presenting it to Molly, induced further *ob-la-deeing* and *ob-la dah-ing,* whereby they wedded, moved to the suburbs, begat children and lived happily, happily ever after. Hoping the song might similarly turn affairs for him, Mr. Emm's brain popped into business power-mode.

"Sell, sell, sell," he chanted like a Gregorian monk, envisioning his daughter's Oxford graduation. When the presentation-hour arrived, Mr. Emm scooped up charts, overheads and his self-confidence and cut a path to the boardroom.

"Manley," Mr. Chilblains said, flanking Mr. Emm in the hallway.

"I'm ready to chip the biscuit into the bucket...cup, Mr. C."

"Might I see you a moment in private?" Mr. Chilblains said, ignoring Mr. Emm's positive missive. Quick to oblige, Mr. Emm followed his boss into the men's room.

"Manley, what in the name of Charles Dickens has gotten into you, or more precisely, what's gotten *onto* you?" Mr. Chilblain queried, his toupée quivering like a furry animal digging a burrow, its hind quarters arching in the air.

"I woke this morning with a bucket on my head, and holding firmly to the belief it will disappear some time today in a manner similar to its extraordinary appearance, but the moment of its vanquishment has not yet arrived. I assure you, however, I am prepared to lure Universal Bucket...excuse me, Universal Biscuit and Food Conglomerate, to our stables."

"The reputation of this firm rests upon your shoulders, Emm...very much like that damned bucket," Mr. Chilblains intoned, placing an executive arm around Mr. Emm's shoulder. Needing no further encouragement and seeing his promotion as clearly as raspberry jam on a crumpet, Mr. Emm adjusted his power-cravat and, with Mr. Chilblains' supportive wishes, puffed out his chest and sallied forth to his mission.

In the boardroom, Mr. Chilblains took his seat, fingers crossed, but as Mr. Emm began his presentation, Mr. Bellend, the CEO of Universal Biscuit and Food Conglomerate, set his water glass on the polished wood conference table, ignoring the coaster there for its pre-determined and express purpose.

"What's with the bucket, Chilblains?" Mr. Bellend said in his standard accusatory tone.

"It's nothing, Mr. Bellend," Mr. Chilblains assured the pompous CEO.

Ignoring the interruption, Mr. Emm set his charts on the rim of the easel and steadied himself for a brilliant exposé, ready to let heave the most capable and persuading advertising sales presentation of his life, the flawless pitch boiling in his brain impressing the coldest executive, had it not been for everyone's preoccupation with Mr. Emm's medieval headdress. His trousers might well have had their fly open, or as said in London artistic circles, "The Victoria and Albert Museum is unveiling a new exhibition," such was the distraction his bucket was making.

Summing his well-conceived and rightly-rehearsed advertising extravaganza, Mr. Emm said slyly, "With Chilblains and Doolap in your corner, Mr. Bellend, Universal Biscuit's success is in the bucket...I mean 'bag'." Emphasizing this critical point, Mr. Emm lifted his foot, stamping the floor and raising his fist to slap the table, but his bucket shifted, and surpassing the table, he lost his balance and listed like the Titanic in its death throes.

At this worst of possible moments, Mr. Emm sneezed, the rupture echoing in his bucket like a depth-charge exploding underwater, Mr. Emm crying out and collapsing to the floor where he lay writhing like a bobby-tasered Tin Man.

Mr. Bellend exploded. "What kind of mockery is this?" he demanded, standing.

"There's been a mistake," Mr. Emm said from the floor. Steadying himself with his arms and sliding his back up the wall, the bucket shrilled against the whiteboard like a flock of screeching water birds taking flight, causing Mr. Emm to moan like a wounded water buffalo.

"Mistake indeed," Mr. Bellend huffed, grabbing his hat and turning to leave.

"Mr. Bellend, I can explain," Mr. Chilblains said.

"We can work this out."

Mr. Bellend reached for a cigar and the doorknob simultaneously. "Explain my ass," he said, whirling his bulbous frame to point a Cubana Giganta-wielding finger in Mr. Chilblains' face. "A man of my stature proposes placing his company's assets with this firm and you and that…that asshole have the nerve to present me with *this*?" Mr. Emm squirmed on the carpet. "It makes a mockery of everything Universal Biscuits stands for," Mr. Bellend railed, shoving the cigar into his mouth and biting down like a pit bull on a poodle's neck. "Biscuits are a serious affair, god-damn-it."

"Mr. Bellend, give me a minute to explain," Mr. Chilblains said.

"Is this your idea of a joke? Are you trying to embarrass my biscuits? What the hell's gotten into you and this buffoon of a marketing person?"

"Mr. B., I mean, Mr. Bellend, we can work this out, I promise," Mr. Chilblains pleaded, the dollar signs in his eyes fading like unmanned ships drifting out to sea.

"That…*ape* has a bucket on his head. Who does he think he's dealing with?" It was a rhetorical question. Mr. Bellend didn't wait for an answer. "I think I can get some straight work out of Munsey, Munsey, Munsey, Sons, Sons and Sons."

"Mr. Bellend, Mr. Emm is our top man. There's been a mix up. If you'd be willing to rethink your position we can take your biscuits to the top." The elevator doors opened and Mr. Bellend stepped in.

"Shove my biscuits up your ass," he said as the doors clammed shut, leaving Mr. Chilblains to suffer the reflection of his impoverished image in their mirrored glass. In the boardroom, Mr. Emm was on his feet and clawing at his cranial constraint like the central figure in Alexander Dumas's *Man in the Iron Mask.*

"This…damn…thing…has…got…to…come…off…*n-n-n-now.*"

Straining like Hercules pulling down a pair of five-foot diameter marble columns, the bucket remained snug as an Egyptian's sarcophagus. Attempting to screw his heavy-duty headgear off, the rigorous action served only to strain his neck. Mr. Emm had just sat down when Mr. Chilblains came in, face wedged between an irritable throat constriction and a massive, pulsing forehead vein, neither of which Mr. Emm was privy to.

"Do you know how much money you've cost this firm?"

"I'll give Mr. Bellend a call in the morning and make this right, Mr. Chilblains.. By then this…*imposition* will have worked itself out," Mr. Emm said like a man sentenced to execution trying to re-assure himself of an eleventh-hour reprieve.

"Oh." Mr. Chilblains stormed out.

"You'll see," Mr. Emm called after him, turning his neck side-to-side to work out the sprain. Picking up his visuals and returning to his cubicle, he was about to burst into a dampened rendition of John, Paul, George and Ringo's *Everybody's Got Something to Hide Except Me and My Monkey* when Regina, the central receptionist, appeared like Dickens' Ghost of Christmases to Come.

"Mr. Doolap wants you in his office."

"Thank you, Regina. I just have to…"

"*Now*." she added sourly.

"Tell him I'll be right in," but Regina was away, failure, like leprosy, driving the untainted to flight.

Mr. Emm clapped his hands. "*O*-kay. Chilblains's smoothed it with Doolap and Doolap wants to discuss an interim plan. Fantastic." Passing Jason on his way to Doolap's chambers, Mr. Emm's janitorial chapeau was praised again.

"It's really a *very* nice bucket, Mr. Emm," Jason said, his forced cheerfulness that of a man watching his best friend being led to the gallows.

"Manley, come in. Sit down. Make yourself comfortable," Mr. Doolap said in a voice as flat and unfeeling as a new measure of asphalt through one of London's posher suburbs. Mr. Emm maneuvered to the requisite chair in front of Mr. Doolap's desk and eased himself into it. Some years ago, he'd attended a workshop in which he learned to use the plural *we* in moments such as this. Clearing his throat, Mr. Emm began.

"What can we do for you, Mr. Doolap?" Mr. Doolap thought Mr. Emm was referring to himself and his bucket.

"Manley," Mr. Doolap said, leaning back in his chair, clasping his hands behind his head and staring at the ceiling as if he'd find the words for which he was searching imprinted there. "You've been an invaluable asset to Chilblains and Doolap throughout the years." He removed his hands from behind his head, leaned forward, opened a box of cigars and took one out, not offering Mr. Emm one to similarly indulge. Clipping the end, he stuck it in his puckered mouth and flicked the lighter on his desk. Thrusting the severed end into the fire, he sucked on it and puffed until a plume of acrid, blue smoke with Mr. Emm's soul in it wafted into the air. Reclining again, he returned his gaze to the ceiling. His vision obscured, Mr. Emm was like a man in a compact sedan who can't see to pass a wide-bodied lorry. Thinking Mr. Doolap might have exited the room, Mr Emm harrumphed, the amplified echo resounding in his bucket. Mr. Doolap continued.

"Everyone here's been grateful for your years of hard work, service and dedication."

"It makes a man feel good to know his efforts are appreciated, Mr. Doolap," Mr. Emm said, speaking to the air about him.

"What I'm trying to say, Manley, is," Mr. Emm leaned in, "the tide has turned for you here. You've become a…" Mr. Emm, was thinking this was the announcement of his long-deserved promotion and was tottering in his chair, hanging expectantly on Mr. D.'s final word, "…liability," further qualifying the intent of the meeting with, "In short, Manley, we're letting you go." Mr. Emm's constitution was that of a nine-pin stunned by a bowling ball delivered with decisive aim and deliberate purpose.

"But Mr. Doolap," Mr. Emm blurted, standing and leaning on Mr. Doolap's desk to keep his shaking legs from collapsing under him. "My career *is* Chilblains and Doolap. It's in my blood. I… I *am* Chilblains and Doolap. I was on the fast track," this last statement being a naïve interpretation of his time at the firm, having been promoted only once, from lower to mid-level management, in nineteen years.

"Very sorry, old boy," Doolap said, disingenuously feigning sympathy. "Due to these economically-down-turned times you'll be receiving a gold-*plated* watch in the mail." It was all Mr. Emm could do to maintain his rapidly diminishing attention on his former employer, his bucket and accompanying dismissal rattling him to his core. Mr. Doolap blew another cloud of grayish-blue smoke.

"Of course your files remain confidential. Do not attempt to remove anything from your office other than your personal effects. Thank you for your efforts and the best of luck in whatever venture you choose. Human Resources will administer a severance check and Security will see you out of the building." Mr. Doolap pushed a standard release-from-work-with-non-competition-clause under Mr. Emm's nose. "Read this and sign it." Slapping the intercom, he barked, "Regina, come in here and take a memo."

"What is this?" Mr. Emm asked.

"Read it," Mr. Doolap ordered as if he'd just lost a million pounds of revenue, which he had.

"I…can't," Mr. Emm said.

"Maybe if you took that damn bucket off your head?"

"No, Mr. Doolap, I mean, I never learned to read."

Mr. Doolap shook his head. "Well, that's grounds to cover our asses if you try to sue. A man who can't read can't be a Chilblains and Doolap man. You've obviously lied to us during selection and that nullifies unemployment compensation and retirement benefits."

Irrevocably maligned in person and pocketbook, Mr. Emm signed the release like a man scribbling a Scotland Yard confession. Passing Regina at the door, notepad and pen in hand, he heard Mr. Doolap begin his dictation: *To all employees of Chilblains and Doolap: As of today, Mr. Manley Emm is no longer an employee of Chilblains and Doolap and furthermore, if anyone sees him on these premises or gives him access..."*

Mr. Doolap's words faded from Mr. Emm's bucket with each mortifying step down the hallway. Emptying his desk, Mr. Emm felt like a Mayan temple-worker prodded to build pyramids 'til he could no longer stand only to find himself between two security guards hell-bent on removing his heart as well as his physical aspect from the building.

"Five minutes, Mr. Emm," the taller, thinner guard said.

Lost in the horrific image of his beloved Zoonie's Oxford education morphing into a two-year-associate-business-college-dental-assistant certificate, Mr. Emm didn't answer, picturing his daughter with a six-year-old's teeth clenched to her tender hand. His dignity evaporated, he would've licked the marble flooring in the company entryway for it to be yesterday again. He would've sucked pigeon droppings off the Peter Pan statue in Hyde Park if it could've changed the last thirty minutes. No longer a man with only a bucket on his head, his psyche was a ruptured sewer main, his ego a jagged and gaping fault-line, his financial future a black hole that had sucked his self-confidence to provide for his family into an uncertain abyss. At thirty-nine years of age, in four words, *Mr. Emm was screwed.*

Boxing the length and breadth of his Chilblains and Doolap tenure, he imagined himself a modern-day Samson ripping out the confining walls around him, bringing the entire building crashing down. What he opted for was a memo, written by Jason who'd been instructed to present Mr. Emm's severance check. Tears in their eyes, Mr. Emm spoke and Jason wrote:

Employees of Chilblains and Doolap, I make my exit with fondest memories of this hallowed firm, but also with a profound sadness, trusting each of you will continue to push onward and upward in your endeavors. I wish you the best of luck in everything. May you one and all find the good fortune you seek. Making my humble exit, I remain, sincerely yours, Mr. Manley Emm, Former Assistant Senior Mid-Level Manager.

Jason held the piece of paper aloft as Mr. Emm tilted his head to visualize the results of their combined efforts. With *The Long and Winding Road* playing as the soundtrack to his abrupt departure, Mr. Emm seized the memo and ripped it to shreds, tossing its pieces in the air. Jason respectfully retreated, giving Mr. Emm the necessary physical and emotional space to complete his review and subsequent tirade.

"Son-of-a-bitch," Mr. Emm fumed, snapping his Chilblains and Doolap fountain pen in two.

Observing this flagrant outburst of mayhem and misuse of company property, the guards interpreted Mr. Emm's defiance as utterly frank sabotage and thereby, a terrorist threat. Having been thoroughly trained and drilled in anti-insurgent methods for such an occasion, the taller guard mashed Mr. Emm's face flat against the wall, spread-eagling and immobilizing the rest of Mr. Emm while the other guard retrieved the pen pieces as evidence of Mr. Emm's insurrectional behavior. Forcing his arms behind his back, they launched Mr. Emm out of the office and down the hall through the common area to the elevators, Jason facilitating the expulsion of Mr. Emm's office belongings as if the box contained the axe with which Mr. Emm's head was to be summarily departed from his person in swift order. Escorted from the building and released to the street, Mr. Emm was handed his things. Jason retreated into the building like a cuckoo-clock bird that had done its job in bang-up fashion, while Mr. Emm listened to the first guard read the statutory repercussions should he set foot on the premises ever again.

A taxicab backfired. Mr. Emm assumed its resonation in his bucket to be the last gasp of his imploding ego, his anger fizzling to an overwhelming sense of nauseating dejection.

Tipping his head to observe his reflection in the smoked-glass panes of Chilblains & Doolap's lobby windows, his brain tuned to the familiar Liverpool lyric pertaining to the boy who's *going to carry a weight a long time*.

Kicking the curb and collapsing into a heap, Mr. Emm vocalized his self-contempt with, "Stop singing Beatles' songs. Stop it. Just…stop…it," reminding himself that in less than an hour he'd gone from mid-level management to unemployed sidewalk-sitter-with-a-bucket-on-his-head. "Rat's ass, rat's ass, Christ to Hell and Charing Cross," he swore in vain, slapping the pavement with his hands and feet.

Now, a man sitting on the sidewalk talking to himself and taking the Lord's name and Underground stops in vain is one thing, but a man sitting on the sidewalk talking to himself and taking the Lord's name and Underground stops in vain with a *bucket on his head* is quite another. Mr. Emm did not go unnoticed.

"You there," a police officer interposed. "Stop yeh rubbish-talk and move along."

"I used to work here," Mr. Emm sobbed, finding his way to his feet and pointing at his former place of employment's impersonal edifice. "The bastards tossed me. Nineteen years and they sling me like a side of cold beef." Mr. Emm was hoping for some consolation from the officer.

"Well, yeh can't be yabbering yer fowl derisions hereabouts. If you persist, I'll slap cuffs on yeh and haul yeh to the 'Yard."

"Go screw yourself, you tubby bastard," Mr. Emm blurted, giving the officer cause to make good on his threat. The public servant's billy-club made swift and forceful contact with Mr. Emm's hardware-headgear, the top of which, in turn, made solid contact with the bobby's chin, dropping the officer to the sidewalk.

"Look there," a law-abiding passerby said, pointing at Mr. Emm as if she was identifying Jack the Ripper in a police line-up. "That man's downed a bobby."

Several members of London's business community stepped forward to do what they believed their civic duty, the woman instructing them to, "Hold him fast whilst I fetch reinforcements."

Surmising the rapidly deteriorating scene, Mr. Emm scooped up his cardboard-enclosed personal effects and, with a savage burst of adrenalin, fled the scene, huffing, snarling, darting, dashing and flailing upon coat and cloak of London's employed until making full-frontal contact with a traffic-signal pole, which sent him to the sidewalk as if his pounding heart had been pierced with a silver bullet meant specifically for such a loathsome creature as he had most swiftly become.

Lingering horizontally, Mr. Emm had what Existentialists refer to as an *out-of-body experience*, floating overhead, watching himself from above like in some moody and foreboding Ingmar Bergman film. His once solid world completely shattered, never in his life had he felt so disconnected from humanity. Then a man spoke.

"I say, gov'nuh." A pair of men's shoes bobbed from side to side within Mr. Emm's limited horizontal vision. Shifting his box of belongings from the tuck of his right arm to the tuck of his left, the smell of blood pudding, meat pies, bitters and ales filled his nostrils. "When yeh'll be kickin' th' bucket, yeh won't be havin' far tih go, will yeh?" The shoes cackled, rocking on their heels unsteadily and holding that position like a surfer at the top of a wave.

Peripherally, Mr. Emm spied *two* pairs of shoes stepping up a landing and into an establishment from which the aromas were emanating. Limping like a wounded werewolf, Mr. Emm packed his person and effects into *The Boiled Boar's Head*, removing himself from afflicting public eye.

It being of a late-afternoon hour, three species of bar-goers regularly frequenting such establishments were making concerted headway in enjoyment of their libations, including those partaking of them in orderly fashion about to make their way to other engagements, those drowning their troubles in liquid balm that ultimately would serve to reinforce the original reason for their drinking, and finally those who make imbibing alcohol a rowdy affair, everyone and every thing in their perimeter becoming fodder for prankish social-antics.

"Here's a fellow with a lot on his mind," one of the third types said, mocking Mr. Emm's preposterous appearance in splendid blackguard fashion.

"Or at least a lot on his head," a fellow reveler

buffooned, giving Mr. Emm a tangibly inspired ribbing, the barroom rapidly taking on the boisterous ambiance of a post soccer-match crowd. Stung from being the brunt of this line of jest, at the same time Mr. Emm felt spritzed with merriment at being included in the banter. Spotting an expanded waistline, white shirt and black-tie opposite him at the bar, he rightly assumed the bartender had arrived.

"See here, good man, I'd like a snifter of your finest brandy," Mr. Emm said with as much aplomb as he could muster.

Someone shouted, "Ask 'im if 'ee wants a mop to go with 'iz bucket," the pub-crowd exploding into a rousing rendition of Monty Python's *Always Look On The Bright Side Of Life*. A swift and emphatic hand-pat to his shoulder nearly disrupted Mr. Emm's delicate maneuvering of the jigger of de Valcourt Napoleon VSOP he was attempting to steer towards his mouth. Steadying himself, Mr. Emm lifted the tumbler, tucked the glass under the bucket's rim and let the sweet aroma and soothing effect of the invigorating elixir erase his demoralizing woefulness. This first brandy positively modifying his demeanor, Mr. Emm ordered a second, third, fourth then fifth, conducting spirited renditions of *Yellow Submarine, With a Little Help From My Friends,*

When I'm Sixty-Four, We Can Work It Out and *Penny Lane*, ending with an encore of *With a Little Help From My Friends*.

Beatles, brandy and several hours of robust and raucous revelling proving a heady mixture, Mr. Emm was poured into a coach with his address exacted from his wallet and pinned to his lapel, whereupon he was delivered to his darling missus. Diagnosing his inebriated condition, Mrs. Emm straightaway put her husband to bed.

Early next morning the phone rang and Mrs. Emm summoned her husband to entertain the caller's entreaties. Mr. Emm picked up the phone and snugged it between his ear and shoulder under the bucket's rim.

A voice on the other end said, "Monsieur Emm?"

"That is I," Mr. Emm admitted, his voice activating a sickening pounding in his head.

"You may recall zat we spoke last eve-en-ning in zee Boar's Head. I am zee Frenchman zat wanted to know about your bucket. You were a beet *gilled*, I think you say here in your country."

Having no recollection whatsoever of any such conversation, but not wanting to admit most of the previous evening was a blur, Mr. Emm said, "Yes, I remember it quite clearly."

Sensing Mr. Emm might be in denial as to his recalling the previous evening's escapade, the monsieur said, "I gave you my card. You put eet in your left suit-coat pocket."

"Could you hold a moment?" Mr. Emm rummaged the pockets of yesterday's coat and retrieved a white business card with simple black lettering that read: *Monsieur Jean–Marie Teabag, Les Technologies Teabag Toiletical.* "Monsieur Teabag," Mr. Emm crooned into the receiver.

"*Oui.*"

"What can I do for you?" The smell of financial sustenance arm-wrestled the odor of stale brandy permeating his cranial enclosure.

"You av an oo-nique situation, Monsieur Emm. I know cleaning products, and in all my years, I av never zeen any-zing like it."

"I'm just a man with a bucket on his head," Mr. Emm said, bluffing an unaffected demeanor to match this astounding revelation.

"But zat iz where you are wrong, Monsieur."

"A minor inconvenience that will work itself out presently."

"Oh, eet's more zan zat, Monsieur. Eet's a Berkman 147 Specially Ionized 29-H."

"Ay?" Mr. Emm said, not knowing buckets from biscuits. *Yesterday* he'd have told everyone he *knew* biscuits. Today, he wasn't so certain.

"But zat iz not ze peculiar part. Ze unusual zing eez ze serial number. It should not eg-zeest."

"How do you mean?"

"Monsieur Emm, when bucket companies number and letter zare products zey do so according to date of production."

"And?"

"Your serial number eez for a bucket zat duz not eg-zeest. Yours eez for a date in ze *foo-ture*."

Mr. Emm hesitated. "It's a mistake is all." Yesterday he was a man with a bucket and the weight of the world on his shoulders. Today he was being told his head did not yet exist.

"Eet's sur-real-ee-stee-cly synchro-nee-stique to find a man wif' a bucket on his head, but eet iz sheer science feek-shun for eet to av a serial number from ze foo-ture."

Ready to end the conversation, Mr. Emm gave the caller one more chance to make sense. "And your point?"

"Monsieur Emm, I would like you to come work for me. I am expanding to England and with you as ze figurehead so-to-speak, I sink we might, excuse ze pun, 'clean up'."

Mr. Emm clarified his position with total silence.

"Monsieur Emm, thees opportunity eez absolutely amazing for uz both. Who would av thought zat a man with a warehouse full of mops would cross zee Channel from Calais to Folkestone, wander into a London pub and meet a man weef a bucket on eez 'ead?"

Sensing something financially profound within his grasp, Mr. Emm cleared his throat. "Good things happen to good people," he said, discounting yesterday's termination from Chilblains and Doolap while eating his last morsel of humble-pudding. *Given what's transpired in the previous twenty-four hours, is this the pot of gold at the end of Misfortune's raincloud? Maybe I'm holding a winning hand after all*, he thought. *I've a good head on my shoulders, even if it's got a bucket fit snug to it.* Laying the receiver down, he looked in the direction of the mirror, wondering what contrivances he would have to tell his wife until he could be certain what he was hearing wasn't a liqored-and-Liverpooled fantasy.

"Daddy?" It was Zoonie outside the bedroom door.

"Yes, pumpkin."

"May I come in?"

"Certainly, cupcake. Come right in."

"The door's locked."

Leaping across the room, he jammed a toe on the bedpost.

"Oooooooow." He opened the door.

"Daddy, are you alright?"

"I most certainly am, dear."

"I hope you don't mind."

"Mind?"

"The face."

"The face?"

"Despite being convinced you and mother purposely embarrass me to my friends, I've decided to show my support for all the hard work you do in providing for us, and I painted a smiley-face on your bucket."

Mr. Emm raised his hands to his head.

"Do you like it?"

"Fetch the hand-mirror from your mother's *boudoir*," he said, and receiving it, positioned himself so he could see the visage reflected in tandem from the hand and wall mirrors; his bucket was adorned with a prominent yellow and black smiley-face.

"Super," he said.

"If you have to wear that bucket for the rest of your life, I want you to be happy."

Mr. Emm, feeling like a cripple who's just been told

by his doctors he'd never walk again, sprang to his feet to dance a jig. Snapping up the phone, he agreed to meet Monsieur Teabag at the new London headquarters of *Les Technologies Teabag Toiletical* the following Monday.

Passing Saturday and Sunday reading and choring, on Monday Mr. Emm dressed and left the house as usual, his wife and daughter vowing to press on despite whatever familial handicap the bucket might bring. Tramming the Underground and finagling a double-seat to himself again, he clung to the business card Monsieur Teabag had given him. Entering the imposing high-rise without incident, he made his way to the main office.

"We weesh you to feel comfortable 'ere, Monsieur Emm. You are ze figurehead and your dee-sire iz our bee-ding," Monsieur Teabag reassured him from across a massive, wooden desk. If Mr. Emm still felt like a man in a wheelchair, it was solid gold and turbo-charged.

Sales soared seismically, launching Mr. Emm along with Teabag Toileticals on an astoundingly successful ride. Several months in, Mr. Emm felt secure enough to tell his wife and daughter how he'd been let go from Chilblains and Doolap, how it was his further misfortune to be shunned and hunted like a desperate animal through the streets of London, how he serendipitously came to meet Monsieur Teabag, the following morning to be told of his fabulous turn of fate and how over the past several months he'd forged their future and reclaimed the family's dignity. Confessing his mistrust of financial institutions and investment firms, he admitted to stashing grand sums about the house. Mrs. Emm ecstatically forgave him, but later that day, her friends over for a study session, Zoonie pulled a pantry drawer open and out plopped packets and packets of banded pound notes. Having filled coffee cans, the mattresses and even the window seat, places to stash gains were running low.

Mrs. Emm advised her husband of the timely need to, "Do something with all this sterling," and made an appointment for him to meet with a financial advisor.

The next day, taking a seat across from the money manager and prepared to hear ways to increase his grand and growing fortune, the fiduciary administrator did not disappoint.

"Mr. Emm. You are certainly well off, but you could be *even more fabulously*-fortuned if you invested some of your wealth. Take a look at this." He handed Mr. Emm a financial prospectus on a piano that could be played under water and waited. "Well, what do you think?" the advisor asked.

"I don't know," Mr. Emm offered hesitantly.

"I didn't ask what you know, Mr. Emm. What do

you *think?*"

Mr. Emm laid the report on the desk.

"Well, you see, I never learned to read."

The financier pushed his chair away from his desk and removed his glasses.

"Mr. Emm, you've obviously done well despite your social handicap, but do you know what you'd be doing right now if you *had* learned to read?"

Without a moment's hesitation, Mr. Emm straightened himself, leaned back in his chair, looked out the window to the streets of London far below and all the people scurrying to jobs that would bring little in the end.

"Collecting a measly pension from Chilblains and Doolap."

Chapter 6

Letter to the Mayor

Mr. Mayor,

Hearty congratulations on the success of your wildlife management program wherein increasingly aggressive park squirrels and chipmunks are rounded up and deprived of their lives by highly-skilled small-animal experts. The meager cost of three quarters of a million dollars per year per exterminator begs the question whether a similar program could be instigated to deter marauding politicians and out-of-control CEOs, bank officials and lobbyists from squeezing the value out of everything they touch. As the monies saved from the squirrel solution have now been re-appropriated to undermining those audacious geese squatting in the town park, we might channel the sixty-five cents of every dollar funneled to Defense and its shadowy, masonic accomplices through anonymous private and corporate bank accounts to addressing the nagging concerns of education, healthcare, sustainability and homelessness. We might even find a pittance to assist that fleeting dove named Peace.

Have your girl contact my girl when you're free to sit down and talk. Some of the residents here at the retirement center said they'd be happy to help. Who doesn't want the chance to bitch-slap a politician and his cronies? Three whacks for five bucks, like at the carnival. My grandkids like the idea.

For your consideration,
Sam Creek, *Citizen Publius*

Chapter 7

The Old River Bridge

The old river bridge was an eyeball-poppin' marvel when first constructed. There'd been nothin' like her in these parts and most everyone agreed there'd be nothin' like her ever again. We was all truly grateful when she finally come in.

She was a one-laner, but fer folks 'round here, half a bridge was better 'n none.

Some of the more fervent pew-packers claimed she was heaven-sent. Reality was taxpayer money and sweat'd got her done. If God was in the equation, he was lyin' in the riverbank shade with a tall can a Packey's in his hand.

The bridge down at Placetown had steel legs in concrete pylons, but ours was of the hangin' variety. Nobody'd've cared if she'd swung from turkey tails as long as it got us 'cross the river without havin' t' go downriver and come back up every time.

Maynard Paxton had a ferry here fer a coupla' years. Ol' Maynard liked t' get drunk as a groundhog and a lot of times nobody'd be there t' run the boat across. The boat'd be there and Maynard'd be there, but he'd be so ground-hogged nobody wanted t' take their chances with him. Maynard was scratchy in the britches 'bout anybody but him piloting his ferry.

Hoisting himself up like a rye-eyed Popeye, he'd announce, "This here's *my* rig, an' um 'er cap'n and nobody but nobody steadies 'er wheel 'ceptin' 'er cap'n," a half-pint of whatever whiskey was on sale at Merchant's Mart peeking out of his vest-pocket like a mouse checkin' t' see if the cat was 'round. He wore a sailor hat on his head and it wobbled like a crow's nest so's no one could tell if it was the hat or his head cocked sideways.

"Thanks, but no thanks," most people'd say an' wave then head down t' Placetown. Some acted like he wasn't there a'tall.

One day Maynard was sailin' higher than Captain Ahab, three sheets-t'-th'-wind passed out on deck. Th' line come untied and him an' his boat floated downriver, hit some rocks and that was all she wrote fer Maynard and his boat. His dog, Banjo, was sittin' on th' bank with that silly sailor hatta his in 'er mouth when Lyle Mintlock found 'er an' everyone realized what'd happened. Lyle took Banjo home with him. Their old boxer'd died in his sleep that spring so it worked out fer all concerned parties, all a' course 'cept Maynard. His body washed up pickled and preserved down at Elliston a week later.

With Maynard an' th' boat gone, we couldn't get 'cross no more. Everybody said there oughta' be a bridge here so folks wouldn't have to go so far outta' their way, but nothin' happened fer a long time. There was talk 'bout a bridge, then some taxes an' more talk an' more taxes. Ya' coulda' built a bridge outta' all th' doughnuts scarfed up at th' county council-meetin's over at the Pentecostal Church o' God. Could'a floated it on the coffee we drank with 'em too. Nothin' got done though.

Between givin' to the church fer what we was s'pposed t' get in the hereafter, givin' to Pepper fer what we'd drank in his bar the week a'fore and givin' to the taxman fer what we was already gettin' screwed outta' by th' government, we weren't gettin' our bridge, an' we was jus' about all given out on givin' out.

Our County Representative, the fat and famous Farley Maverick, promised a new bridge in turn fer re-election. Farley wasn't always fat, and he wasn't always County Representative. When he was store clerk at Merchant's Mart, he was husky. Then he bought th' Rep job from a friend of an in-law that had a relative in office in need of retirin' a'fore th' Law retired him to the state penitentiary. Soon's Farley started talkin' politics, all that bureaucratic hot air stopped up in 'im and he got whatcha' call big and burly. All them fast food joints up in the capital and him sittin' on his county seat all the time turned his burliness down-right lardy.

Farley could chew a pastry on the right side of his mouth an' whistle down the middle while explainin' out the lef' how wonderful somethin' was goin' t' be, all without stoppin' t' breathe. Folks 'round here said how they wanted to get rid of their coal stoves an' have Farley sit on their sofas all winter blowin' hot air. When he couldn't get any bigger without explodin', everyone started callin' him Skim Milk because his hands was always skimmin' somethin' offa' somethin'. He thought his nickname was a sign of affection, like yeh call a big man Tiny.

Farley was good fer nothin' 'cept a beer 'n' a shot 'er two at Pepper's 'roun' 'lection time. He'd slap you on the back an' make yeh spill yer beer an' knock yer cigarette ash on th' table. One time Riley Bowman told him, "Buy me a shot, yeh swindler, 'er I'll vote for th' other bastard." Farley was always obligin' when folks talked plain an' t' the point like 'at.

Then after one 'lection we got our bridge. Turns out

the new Lieutenant Governor's mother-in-law lived up at Langton an' he finagled so's a new bridge went in here so's his wife's mother didn't have to go down to Placetown no more. The squeaky wheel got greased with somethin' other than Farley's lousy hair tonic. Farley took credit fer it anyway.

"That's th' hard work of yer County Representative, Farley 'Skim Milk' Maverick, workin' fer his constituents." It was funny hear 'im call himself 'at, like it was a badge of honor or somethin'.

"Tell it to th' lieutenant governor's mother-in-law, yeh fat bastard," Tom Glassleen shouted from th' back. Helpful suggestions like that rolled off Farley like water from a duck's butt, but it finally happened. We got our bridge. Government engineers wearin' lime-green overalls drivin' orange pick-ups come down from Fairmount. Deer hunters, we called 'em. Long haulers with I-beams, steel cables and pontoons showed up like ants at a picnic. 'Even 'coptered in a crane on a boat. When any of us wasn't workin' or huntin' we'd go down t' watch or sit in front of Merchant's Mart an' talk 'bout how wonderful life was gonna' be when th' bridge got in.

'Problem was the river here ain't right fer a bridge with legs so's they made ours the suspension kind, a marvel of its time. Wouldn't yeh know, soon's it went in, one uh th' Hazlett girls took her life an' that of 'er unborn child by jumpin' off our bridge. 'Shame.

Like an opened floodgate, our bridge became a magnet fer anybody with a short-term problem lookin' fer a long-term answer. There was a year in there we had thirteen jumpers. One fool missed th' water, hit th' mud an' lef' his body outline two feet deep. When th' mud dried, his relatives put plaster over th' impression. 'Tried to make the cast a tourist attraction. Charged folks a quarter to see it. Next flood washed it away an' that was 'at. Alotta' folks thought th' Devil's will was our bridge's bittersweet curse.

She'd served 'er purpose for many years, a slang of governors 'n' their lieutenants an' mothers-in-law come 'n' gone. Our marvel of wonder'd become a wheezer of woebegone days. Her fresh, government-gray went ratty, rusty brown, like th' economy. Her boards'd cracked an' rotted an' th' nails come loose. Our Little Lucy'd seesaw like a pony on a merry-go-roun' when anyone crossed her.

There've been shacks up in these hollers that've burned down, fell down, been knocked down or jus' fallen apart, but ole Lucy kept hangin'. Sagged in the middle when nobody was on her an' sagged fiercer when a coal truck inched over. Kenny Woodwart, one of th' younger foremen who married into th' mine, said he had a dream 'bout takin' his family across an' she collapsed. He heard th' boards breakin' an' his wife an' kids screamin' an' swore he wouldn't cross her no more. That story got aroun' an' scared th' bejesus outta' people, so's folks started goin' down t' Placetown, sayin' Little Lucy weren't worth dyin' fer an' there we was where we'd been all them years a'fore.

Th' faithful said God would keep Lucy up 'til th' new one went in, hopin' like th' rest of us sinners she wouldn't come down with any of us on 'er. Church service would end an' them ole boys'd stand aroun' takin' bets on when she'd go.

There was a picturesque aspect to 'er even durin' 'er declinin' years. She was pretty t' look at when th' sun hit 'er in a postcard way. Th' dirt an' leaves collectin' on 'er made 'er look soft an' invitin', like a calendar girl just past 'er prime.

City folk in their Ess-You-Veez out fer a Sunday ride would come admire 'er and snap photos. It was funny, them in our neck of th' woods. They'd drive out onto ol' Lucy slow, then th' fathers'd take pictures of th' family standing 'roun' th' car smilin,' never realizin' they wuz cheatin' death.

One of our old boys'd yell, "That bridge's a'gonna'

go any minute."

Another'd add, "She's goin' now," an' them city folks'd pack their kids in them city trucks an' haul ass outta' th county.

Consensus was an errant coal truck'd most likely do 'er in. When th' coal trucks started goin' down t' Placetown, rumors flew like shrapnel from one of 'em shoulder-launched Al-Quaeda rockets.

None of us could say we was doin' particularly fine, what with th' economy in a slump an' another war startin' up. Even when th' economy was doin' fine an' we weren't routin' terrorists from them other countries and our banks and corporations, folks up in 'ese hollers just got by, year in, year out, babies born, old folks dyin', younguns gettin' married, preachers sermonin' on Sundays, picklin' our livers at Pepper's anytime we cared to an' relaxin' on the river bank, fishin' pole in one hand, a tall can of Packey's in the other.

Talk 'roun' town'd turn to when a replacement bridge was goin' in an' if it'd go in here or up at Holman's Creek. Th' new governor had relatives up 'at way. Folks was speculatin' 'bout th' new bridge while Lucy contemplated fallin' down of 'er own accord. Th' old-timers joked how them Tal-ee-ban should blow 'er up. Folks get what's goin' on. First th' taxman robs us, then the banks and corporations chew us up and steal as much as they can take, then them Homeland Security fellas pick our bones fer the few remainin' freedoms we have left. All 'at talk 'bout terrorists gettin' us's jus' propaganda so them politicians can do anythin' they please. They have, they do and will continue to.

Th' new County Rep, Farley Maverick's grandson, Grady, was havin' a worse time of it than th' rest of us, what with things not goin' well in general an' at home. His wife, Joanna, she'd givin' him his walkin' papers and showed him th' door. Rumor had it she'd shown him an inch-round plumber's pipe. He was stayin' in his huntin' trailer up by the ol' Hawley Mine, sourer than a crabapple stewin' in its own juices.

'Seein' him in town an' askin' how he was doin', yid be told, "I'm goin' down t' jump off that damn-ol' bridge." Talk 'bout pokin' a pig in th' eye with a stick. Our bridge'd lost its attraction fer bein' a good place t' toss your cares an' people weren't none too happy with Grady fixin' to re-instate its reputation, 'specially him bein' County Rep an' all. Nobody really *believed* him. He'd always been a blabberer. It was genetic, or as some liked to point out, 'all in his jeans.' Nobody liked anyone mentionin' jumpin'.

Grady's orneriness had hit an all-time high. He'd even been eighty-sixed from Pepper's, now owned and operated by Pepper's youngest daughter, Nadine. Grady'd drove his Bronco through 'er screen door.

"Tweren't on purpose," he claimed. "I skidded on that damn loose gravel." He'd only pushed th' frame a little and bent the metal jamb an inch, but Nadine'd had enough and went off like a rooster on a rooftop. She told him to stay out or she'd sic 'er daughters on 'im. Bein' eighty-sixed from Pepper's was like bein' excommunicated from church, which would bother most of us a lot less than being eighty-sixed from Nadine's. Only thing worse than havin' one of Nadine's daughters sicced on yeh was havin' *both* sicced on yeh. That was tantamount to goin' to hell while still alive.

Her daughters was professional, hardcore, hillbilly waitresses with jus' th' right balance of humor, pathos and pugilistic skills. Th' older daughter, Eileen, had a solid forearm. One time some rowdy-redneck fellas stepped over th' line an' Eileen laid 'em flat, bashed 'eir noses so hard they had t' smell outta' their ears.

The younger one, Rita, would pick up anything handy and hit yih on the head with it. Funny thing was them fellas' would 'pologize on th' spot or next day after they'd come to, an' they always come back. There was no place else t' go. Placetown was too far. If a person wants t' pickle his liver in these parts, he has got t' go t'

Nadine's.

Pepper'd been real estate smart, puttin' his bar between the mine an' town. Location, location, location, ain't that what they say? Yeh got too drunk, Pepper'd have Nadine drive yeh home. Now Nadine has her daughters doin' the same, our own little hillbilly-taxi service.

Grady'd dragged that beat-up huntin' trailer of his up t' th' ol' Hawley Mine over on Royalton Ridge. Th' toilet was torn out, an' there was no heat, gas or 'lectricity. It was only good for sittin' in, drinkin, an' waitin' fer a turkey or deer to come through, but it was Grady's castle. He claimed he was up 'ere 't think,' which is ironic a'cause Grady's not what yeh'd call a thinkin' man, other than thinkin' how he could dip his hand in public money. His reputation as a politician was flounderin' like a fish floppin' under our Little Lucy. Rumor was this would be his last time a'squeezin' his butt into that county seat.

Grady'd been spendin' an inordinate 'mount o' time out on Little Lucy when he wasn't fightin' with Joanna to let 'im come home t' her 'n' th' kids 'n' 'er mother 'n' his wife's sister, or grovelin' fer Nadine to let 'im back in th' bar.

"Dear Jesus, give me a sign or I'm jumpin'," yeh'd hear th' crazy bastard holler. It was like he was playin' chicken with 'at bridge, haulin' out on 'er and squealin' to a stop, gettin' out and jumpin' up an' down, talkin' to himself.

"Jump or drive, yeh silly bastard," people would shout.

Grady was lookin' fer a sign harder'n he was headin' fer th' hereafter 'cause fer all his whoopin' and hollerin', he hadn't jumped. Fact was, he was an embarrassment. When strangers'd see him dancin' aroun' on that bridge, they'd hit reverse and high-tail it outta' town. If Grady hadn't married Sheriff Neeley's daughter, he'd a' been put away like nobody's business long ago.

One Sunday my wife, Emma, said, "Joanna asked if yeh'd talk to Grady an' tell him he can come home if he calms down, stops drinkin' an' runnin' 'round talkin' an' actin' like a crazy man and starts goin' t' church again. He's yer friend."

Emma and Joanna'd been in Church Club together long afore Grady inherited his political position an' as I was th' only person still talkin' to him, I got singled out as's friend.

Dammit.

It was November an' it smelled like snow comin'. Emma'd took th' grandkids t' church. Spooner, th' grand-daughter of one of Banjo's grand-daughters, was holed up at the trailer with Grady. Grady'd taken Spooner after Lyle Mintlock passed away. Spooner was so blind, deaf an' feeble, yeh had to touch 'er to let 'er know you was there. She'd jump like a scared rabbit, wheeze hard an' nearly fall down. Poor gal was plagued with arthritis from 'er head to 'er hips. I went up t' talk Grady outta' his hell-hole, but Grady wasn't there, just Spooner, so I drove to Pepper's, now Nadine's. It was th' Sunday after th' Monday we'd been told our local government'd decided t' foil th' Taliban's chance at another easy target. Th' county was takin' Lucy down with dynamite.

Comin' off th' mountain, I joined a line of trucks an' cars backed up from th' bridge. Grady's was first in line where Little Lucy'd been, but was no more.

"Here's 'at sign yeh been prayin' fer," Ranny Watson yelled, which, t' a man that's been drinkin' for two weeks straight an' lookin' for a sign from God, seems soberin' words. Our bridge was gone in a cloud of dust an' Grady was starin' down 'at its rubble. As much as people'd talked 'bout it, nobody'd thought it'd happen.

"Praise the Lord," Grady exclaimed, droppin' t' his knees, one hand holdin' th' hood of his pickup and th' other up in the air like he was swattin' flies or tryn'a touch the face-uh Jesus. Grady thought he'd witnessed a miracle when what he was in the presence of was rotted wood, rusted steel an' an empty case of Packey's.

I got out an' walked down t' talk t' him. Little Lucy was lyin' in the river on her side, cracked in th' middle, but serene an' peaceful like Maynard Paxton passed out drunk on his ferry, water backin' up behind her. Sheriff come an' pulled out a bull horn an' some yellow an' black crime-scene tape an' instructed everybody t' stay back, sayin', like in th' movies, "There's nothin' t' see here, folks," but there *was* somethin' to see, Little Lucy lyin' on 'er side down there in th' river like she'd finally jumped 'erself.

"Take him home, will yeh?" Sheriff Neeley said.

Tears in his eyes, Grady was tryin' to convince me he'd had no hand in Little Lucy's demise. He admitted he'd been feelin' th' Devil in him lately, but he swore up an' down her demise was not of his doin'. That eased my mind. I drove him home and he wailed like a baby, kissin' his kids 'til they wanted t' run outside an' wash the slobber off in a rain barrel.

Th' new bridge's been in a year now. Sheriff Neeley put up a 'No Loitering' sign. 'Guess it's workin'. Nobody's jumped yet.

Emma, the grandkids an' me, we drove up t' Rachel Warton's weddin' t' some fella over in Skawpunk. Th' minister performin' th' ceremony was th' newly-ordained Reverend Grady Maverick. Grady'd learned preachin' from a correspondence school an' now all he wanted to talk about was th' Lord. That was th' biggest drawback to his conversion. As big an asshole as politics made him, religion'd made him an even bigger one. He did a good ceremony. 'Almost forgot th' rings though.

Afterwards, at th' reception, th' bride an' groom cut th' cake, Rachel tossed 'er garter an' bouquet an' everybody danced with th' bride fer a dollar an' done their shot of Old Turkey with th' groom. We was packin' up th' grandkids when I heard our Reverend Grady sobbing himself sick. He'd doe-see-doed a few too many turns with The Gobbler an' was wailin' 'bout how he'd never be able t' make up fer th' sins he'd committed in 'is life. Cryin' an' actin' like a fool, Grady was a slithery otter slidin' down a slippery slope, claimin' he was goin' down t' th' new bridge t' ask fer another sign.

I packed th' grandkids in the truck, meanin' t' get outta' there before I was appointed the official friend of th' spiritually-challenged Reverend Grady 'The Gobbler' Maverick. Pulling th' truck 'roun', I told Emma we should be gettin' while th' gettin' was still good.

On th' way home, I see'd a fella standin' on th' bridge starin' at th' water. Not recognizin' him as anybody from 'roun' here, I hollered, "Jump er join th' priesthood." Th' grandkids stopped flappin' their hands out th' windows an' makin' airplane sounds. Emma'd nodded off. She jerked awake. I apologized fer frightenin' her like 'at. Lookin' in the rearview, I seen th' bridge-stander watchin' us like we was all crazy. He reminded me of Grady. I got goose bumps.

By th' time we got home an' put the grand-kids t' bed, it was dark. It was a nice night so Emma an' me sat on th' porch swing a spell. The moon was full an' made everything an' our bridge glow. We snuggled, watchin' th' stars like we hadn't fer a long time 'til a mournful howl drifted up from th' direction of the bridge, like somethin' wasn't sittin' right with one of Mack David's hounds.

"I hope he gets it straight," I said, "'cause I'm not drivin' down t' talk 'im off."

We hugged an' Emma gave me a big kiss.

Chapter 8

Cleaning Up After the Dead (Death and the Cleaning Girl)

Lower Manhattan was out of the area she normally worked, but Petra Mandovic (*Man*-duh-vich) needed rent, so she took the job. Brown-eyed, mousy-haired, barely five-foot on her toes, Petra knew how to clean houses. She'd been doing it since she was nineteen and attending The National Academy in New York City. Petra Mandovic knew how to clean houses and how to paint in the abstract expressionist style.

Housecleaning afforded her the luxury of working for herself, preserved the flexible schedule a struggling artist needs and allowed her to choose her clientele as much as they chose her. After Prague, Amsterdam and Havana, The Big Apple was an expensive slice of pie, so against her conscience she took the cleaning job across the Hudson River in Montclair, New Jersey. The referral was from one of her regular clients, a gay couple in the

West Village.

She rode the subway to the West 40's, caught a bus through the Lincoln Tunnel and the rest of the way, asking herself if it was worth the travel time. Considering blowing the job off, she arrived in Montclair ready to spend the next three hours housecleaning, and then to rush home and pay the last of this month's rent. Walking the streets lined with row after row of gaudy two-story mansions, she wondered why anyone would have a house so big they couldn't clean it themselves. Her one-room studio in the Bowery was sufficient. The place was icy cold in the winter, but the window faced north, its neutral light perfect for painting.

The house was a behemoth, capable of sheltering eight families of modest means. If it had been hers, she would have started an artist colony, inviting everyone she knew to live there and there'd still be enough square footage for work-spaces and a gallery: the only problem was its suburban location. She could take the city and the country, but anything in between was 'death by suburb,' the place normal people go to give their dreams every opportunity to die.

A head poked from between the window curtains beside the front door as she walked up the stone pathway, but no one appeared at the front door to let her in. Petra clanged the oversized brass knocker and waited. No response from inside.

Thinking it hadn't been a good idea after all, she was about to leave when the cathedral-sized portal opened. A maudlin, matronly woman wearing too much make-up, jewelry and perfume greeted her. Ushering the abstract expressionist in, the biddy launched into a crackling, emotionless diatribe against allowing strangers admittance, followed by a detailed explanation of what was expected of hired help.

Petra listened, nodding when necessary, thinking it odd how people who didn't clean would describe in detail how they wanted it done. She didn't need cleaning explained, and something told her that being here was wrong. Needing the money, she disregarded what intuition was telling her. The crone droned on.

"These knick-knacks will need careful dusting," pointing at two gold-trimmed, track-lit, floor-to-ceiling, glass-handled cabinets crammed with tacky *objets de curiosité*. "Take each one out, dust it, dust the space it rests on, then return it to exactly where it was." She mimicked the instructions as if speaking to a deaf person.

One more layer of make-up and she can take first place in a Tammy Faye Baker look-alike contest, Petra thought, *faux*-politely acknowledging the geezerette's threats with a curtsy, hoping her deference would silence the matriarch so she could get to work, finish and flee to the safety and sanity of Manhattan.

"This chandelier is *quite* expensive. I wouldn't want to be the one who damages it. Hold it steady and don't snag the prisms or they'll break," she said, her tone a mixture of dare and damnation.

Fantasizing knocking the old bat to the ground and pouring drain-cleaner down her esophagus, with a nod Petra masked her eagerness to get started and be done.

The woman cleared her throat with a gargly rasp then turned to face a massive, dark-wood bureau, her elephantine-hoop earrings cutting the air in malevolent Grim-Reaper-scythe arcs.

To clarify their relative social positions, the woman said, "This bureau is *very* old and *very* valuable. Don't lean on it." Opening the top, left drawer, she presented a letter-sized envelope. "Your money," she said succinctly, placing it on the bureau. Inspecting the contents of her lacy, black, over-sized purse, the maternal head-of-household slid a bony arm through the woven handles as if her bag was an automatic rifle and she was unlatching the safety. "I'll be gone three hours. Do a good job and I'll refer you to my friends," she said, walking out and closing the door like the lid on an unidentified person's coffin.

Infuriated by the ghoul's vindictive innuendo, Petra was thrilled with the prospect of the woman's exit until the door opened enough to admit an emaciated index finger pointing at a door at the end of the dim hallway. "I almost forgot. My mother's in there. Do what you can and clean around her. She isn't well. Three hours." The shriveled appendage withdrew before Petra had a chance to hack it off, the front door wheezing shut with finality.

It was as if the woman had jammed a knife in Petra's pride. There'd been no mention of a decrepit mother when she'd agreed to the job. Arms crossed and leaning on the ancient-looking bureau defiantly, Petra squinted dagger-eyes down the shadowy hall.

The abstract expressionist was pissed.

It was maddening cleaning a room with someone in it. Petra envisioned the rheumy-eyed woman studying her every move, plotting to make it look as if the cleaning girl hadn't been thorough, a dirty spoon on a nightstand, a piece of trash on the floor after Petra had gone. She'd been accused of leaving a pubic hair on a Thanksgiving turkey thawing in the kitchen sink. Holding the curly scrap of evidence in her accuser's face, Petra noted it wasn't her color. She'd suspected the husband. He'd made a pass and she'd refused. Middle-aged men liked to fantasize sex with a maid, and if they didn't have a maid, they'd settle for the cleaning girl.

Postponing the ignominy, Petra climbed the wide, carpeted staircase and began work with the master toilet, tub, shower and sinks, counter-tops, mirrors and tiled floor, then the main bedroom, dusting and polishing the furniture and floorboards, making the bed, smoothing the sheets, fluffing the pillows and finishing by vacuuming the carpet. She cleaned the other bathrooms, bedrooms and upstairs common areas, polishing the wood railing and vacuuming the stairs, moving down them backwards one step at a time.

On the main floor she began with the kitchen, cleaning, sweeping and mopping, then the living room, den and study, beginning at the top far corner of each room and finishing with the floor or carpet by the door.

The grandfather clock in the foyer chimed. She'd been working two hours. The only room left was the one with the mother in it. Visualizing a bedridden skeleton reeking of feces and urine, she braced herself for the expected ordeal, dreading being harangued by an older and more addled version of the matron and considered conversational topics she could engage an elderly, infirmed woman with while working around her. Steeling herself, Petra grasped the doorknob, twisted it and pushed.

The room was a morgue, Death lurked in the shadows, waiting to whisk its occupant to the hereafter. Thick, opaque curtains obliterated all outside light. A gust of putrid air brushed Petra's face as it fled the morbid crime scene. Thinking the woman had been mistaken about her mother being in here, Petra discerned a lumped, skeletal outline beneath bed covers and a wasted skull with albino-like skin stretched over it like a freshly-framed canvas propped on an easel of pillows. Tubes projecting from inflamed nostrils and cadaverous hands limp at the woman's sides, a squadron of life-support equipment whirred and hummed like a pit crew working feverishly to figure out why their car won't start. Two vacant blots where eyes should've been telegraphed pain, fear and desperation.

Petra turned away, wanting to bolt from the room, but stepped in, opening the door wide to let in as much light and air as possible.

"Good afternoon," Petra said, imagining herself awaiting death while a younger woman cleaned around her. "I didn't think anyone was here." The woman stared like a dog begging to be let out of its cage.

The invalid's eyes followed Petra, moving to the floor then back to the uncomfortable artist. Raising a withered arm, the corpse wagged an index finger in the air, pointing at Petra in the same manner as the daughter had earlier. Her rotting mouth opened and closed, but no words came out.

She's trying to tell me something, but what?

The index finger flailed, slowly up and quickly down.

"The floor?" Petra asked.

The ghastly head nodded.

"Something on the floor?" They were playing a child's game of twenty questions with life or death as the prize.

Frowning and gurgling, the matriarch lowered then raised her outstretched hand.

"Under the bed?"

The woman nodded.

"Clean under the bed?" Petra said, trying to put her employment into perspective.

The mute head indicated 'no'.

It runs in the family, Petra thought. *Now she's telling me how to do my job.*

The bed-ridden apparition stared at Petra, unwavering.

"What do you want?" Petra demanded, aware she hadn't finished and that time was positioning itself against her.

The dying woman's mouth inflated into a gaping "O" as if blowing ghostly smoke rings, encouraging her soul to escape from her decrepit body. Her index finger curved to a skeletal hook and twitched as if pulling a trigger.

Petra knelt beside the bed and reached underneath to feel smooth wood and cold metal. She pulled it to her, a shotgun. She stood, fist to her mouth.

"I can't."

The woman groaned. Her lips thinned to a livid smile. Her eyes closed in calm entreaty.

"No," Petra insisted. cleaning at a frenzied pace, using all her willpower not to look at the woman.

The specter drew a rattling breath, grabbed the sides of the bed and rocked, as if trying to release the spring that would free her from her mortal coil.

Finishing, Petra moved to the door, wanting to convey she understood, but couldn't fulfill the woman's last wish. Looking at the machines, she tried to conceive how long this woman could wait imprisoned in a rotting corpse, then laid the shotgun on the woman's chest and slid both barrels into her eager mouth. Petra saw her as a baby suckling her mother's breast, as a young girl closing her eyes and tilting her head for her first kiss and now, begging Death and the cleaning girl to be merciful.

As she positioned the woman's thumbs on the triggers, the clock, the machines, the death-rattle in the woman's chest, all ceased and both women began to cry, the abstract expressionist from sadness and pity, the gnarled grandmother with joy and acceptance.

Closing the woman's eyes, she gazed at the appalling sight one last time then walked out of the room, closing the door behind her. Double-barreled desperation pushed her down the hall. Grabbing the envelope from the bureau, she ran from the house and down the driveway. As her feet touched the sidewalk, she heard the percussive boom and seraphic echo, muffled by thick, opaque curtains.

Sniffling tears and having done the most thorough housecleaning of her life, the explosion awakened her, the muses in her head unveiling an onslaught of images demanding to be set on canvas. All that would be required would be to pick up the brush. Her hands would be directed as they had a minute ago.

Petra vowed never to take a cleaning job outside Manhattan ever again.

Chapter 9

Blood Money

Yeh get twenny dolluhs da' first time yeh come an' twenty-five da' second if yeh comes two times in a week. If yeh does it eight times in a month, dey gives yeh an extra ten dollars. Ain't dat some shit? Dey sticks yeh wiff a needle fat as a straw in da' same spot two times a week fuh four weeks and gives yeh a lousy ten dolluhs. Den dey go an' sell da' stuff fuh a hundred and eighty-five dollars a pint. Dat's Cap'talism at work ah'right.

Muh left arm's muh twenny dolluh arm. Muh right's muh twenny-five dolluh one.

Yeh got a vein dat twists like muh left, dey call it a Gumby. Stick a Gumby 'nuf an' yeh'll have a hard time gettin' dat hole tuh stop bleedin'. Den yeh ends up wiff blood all over da place. 'Dey bandage yeh when you done. Yeh rolls down yer sleeve an' walks out, yeh feels dis warm trickle runnin' down yehr ahm, yeh look an' it's *yer* blood makin' a fuckin' mess.

Dey gives yeh auntie-co-ag-u-lant when thuh'r returnin' yeh blood. Dat's what dey calls dat stuff 'at keeps yeh blood from clottin'. Uh thought uh'd steal a couple bags 'n' sell 'em, but dey ain't no good fuh nothing 'cept gettin' blood outta' clothes and keepin' it fum clottin'. Nobody think 'bout dat, not even a junkie. If it's cold out like t'day 'n' yeh bleed on yehsef an' have ta wash yeh shirt and coat, walkin' around wiff a wet sleeve, yeh screwed.

When deys checkin' yeh in, dey marks yer left index-fingernail wiff invisible ink dat shows up unner da' black light. Disco pinky, dey calls it. Dat's so's yeh don' try donatin' at annudder center. Get caught, yeh busted. 'Can't donate nowhere no more.

Muh boyfrien' 'n' me, we was goin' to duh center on Forbes. Doze folks workin' dere be mean. Dey loses yeh file den makes yeh sit fer hours an' don' even tell yeh why. Ac' like it's yer fault. Take two juices aft-uh-wuhds, dey ac' like yeh tryna' rob 'em blind, like dey gonna' go broke yeh took two juices. Uh takes two packets uh crackers once. Dey comes runnin' af'er me like uh was a goddamn terrorist. Dey watches yeh on cameras.

One lady, she works dere, she always drunk. Ev'body knows she can't do nuffin' right. Dey talks behin' her back, take bets fer when she gonna' fuck up and kill somebody, stab somebody's ahm an' make 'em bleed tih deaf.

Now we goin' over ta Lawrenceville. We tryna' get it so's we c'n move over dere. We been stayin' on Bedford Street, up on de Hill, but dey's a buncha' crazy niggahs up dere. Muh best friend, Shawante (Shuh-*won*-tay), she let us sleep in her car oth'uh night. She ain't got no room fer nobody else in her place. Got a houseful heh'seff, babies comin' out her ass.

Picksburgh's alright, but too damn cold. Hell, maybe we moves back to Jacksonville, Florida, or New Orleans. Uh got family dere.

When dey interviews you, dey axe, "You prepared to donate today? You eat a big meal?" Uh always wants to tell 'em, "If we could afford a big meal, would we be sellin' plasma?" Am uh right? Damn straight.

Dey jab yeh finger, take yeh blood pressure, weight, temp-ur-cher an' ever'thing got tuh check out, protein levels, hem-a-do-crits and udder names like characters in a goddamn Greek tragedy. Dey axe if you ever live in Africa. What the hell am uh goin' do in Africa? Deys enough black folk right here. Dat's some silly shit.

Las' Friday, dey tol' dis white dude he couldn't donate 'cause somethin' wrong wiff him. His face all beat up. Yeh could see how much dat twenny woulda' meant.

We all livin' pay-check to pay-check, but if yeh de government, yeh just prints money an' buys every goddamn thing yeh wants. Piss it away's what dey do.

Udder day uh got a interview fer a waitress job. Dey axe me fer a resumé, fer Chrissake. Can yeh believe dat? A resumé to be a waitress, like it rocket science'r sumthin'. While dey interviewin' me fer da job, uh tries to hide mah ahms an' don't know where to look. Muh boyfriend, he say uh shoulda' looked 'em right between duh eyes. 'Didn't want to stare 'em down or be lookin' at de floor alla' time.

Den dey axe me, "What was the last book you read?" Den dey axe, swear to God, "If you wuz an animal, which animal would you be and why?" like dey was playin' 'roun' on der lunch break. Iz a coffeehouse wiff a goddamned bookstore. How come uh have tuh be able tuh read, and what's dat animal bullshit got tuh do wiff anything? It don' matter. 'Didn't get de job anyway.

When dey calls you tih go in back, don't try tih eat or sleep or lift your knees or use a cell phone. Somebody hollers at yeh if yeh do. One a dem hollers at me ag'in, um gonna' slap 'em up silly.

Dey have a VIP system where yeh c'n trade in a DVD an' yeh don't got tih wait in line. You gets what dey call a VIP card. Dey keep duh video, but sometimes it's worth it. Uh seen several layin' dere behind the counter and uh was gonna' reach over an' take 'em, but uh was too scared. Don' wan' teh fuck up so's uh can' donate no more.

Most of de movies dey show're dem slasher movies, or everybody's a vampire bitin' somebody. Dey say da movies can' have no sex-u-al content. If dere was no sex, dere'd be nobody to donate plasma fer all'a duh people gettin' slashed in da slasher movies.

Shit, uh needs a cigarette.

Lizard ain't here today. Dat's what uh calls 'im. He on drugs or somethin'. His tongue move in and outta' his mouth every six seconds. Uh timed 'im. Dat's the kinda shit yeh do laying dere wiff a needle up yeh arm. Lizard, he from some place else. He talk wiff an accent. Las' week, he be readin' *How to Become an Auctioneer*. Good luck talkin' like an auctioneer wiff dat tongue uh his. Blabba, blabba, blabba, sold…right?

'Takes 'bout t'ree hours tih donate, two if yeh lucky. 'Pinches when duh needle go in.

Uh can't wait no more. Gotta' pick up my kids from school. Dey gonna' get an ed-u-ca-tion so's dey don' have to do dis shit.

You got forty cents?

T'anks, baby. Yeh take care now.

Blood Money

Chapter 10

Letter to the Sheriff

Sheriff,

Yesterday at the ball park, my grandson saw five police cars lined up one next to the other, all spread out and angled illegally across twelve parking spaces. He looked at me and said, "Grandpap, why don't police obey the law?"

Having no answer as to why the law applies to some but not others, I let him down…and so did you.

He also noticed police cars coming and going at speeds too fast for where children and families unload and load vehicles. One of these days somebody's going to get plowed over by a cop car.

How about telling your officers to park between the painted lines and to drive at safe speeds like the rest of us? Maybe ask them to obey the law the way they enjoy enforcing it. My one grandson died in Iraq because people jacked with the law and got away with it. I don't want something as bone-headed as that happening here.

With cops doing whatever they feel like anytime they care to these days, a person is hard-pressed to look at the world and see who the good guys are.

For your consideration,
Sam Creek, *Citizen Publius*

Chapter 11

A Very Tall Man with Very Deep Pockets

At seven feet six inches, Nicholas Crockett was a very tall man, not the tallest man in the world, but a damn-sight taller than everyone he met and everyone that met him. Nicholas' aerial advantage owed nothing to his family tree. His grandfather, the tallest person in bloodlineage until him, had towered five-foot-six.

As a child, Nicholas heard the rumor of a midget in his family tree. He'd also been told there was a hunchback and a village idiot among his distant relatives so the midget story bothered him little. Growing up with his vertical estrangement and knowing of these family oddities, he wouldn't have found it amazing to be told there was also a mummy, a vampire and a werewolf lurking among his ancestors, but his singularity led him to attempt to verify or debunk the midget rumor.

At twelve years of age and six feet tall, he found an attic trunk full of letters and photographs, but leafing through the tattered photo albums and perusing shoebox after shoebox of yellow-stained letters contributed nothing substantial for or against the Little Man legend. The letters were jibberish and he didn't recognize the house in the pictures. The other photos only revealed a scruffy array of nondescript strangers refusing to smile under any circumstances.

At eighteen years of age and seven feet in height, for his high school graduation present he traveled by train from his home in Boston to locate extended family in Bloomington, Indiana, in order to learn what he could about his tiny nemesis, but the quest proved futile. Whereas the house in the photographs was on a lively street inhabited by a family on their front porch and milling about their garden, by the time Nicholas got there it was boarded up along with every other building on the street. Considering a transcontinental voyage to investigate family outliers, he dismissed the idea, concluding knowing or not wouldn't make a difference. He was taller than most and midget or no midget, that was that, but what deterred his investigation most was knowing wherever he went he would stand out like a windmill in a strip mall, his fear being that a circus hearing of him would abscond and indenture him as a sideshow freak. He imagined the ringmaster contracting the strong man and bearded lady to follow him and, when the opportunity arose, to conk him on the head and drag him into servitude. Waking dazed and confused with a whopper of a lump on his head to prove he'd not dreamed his unfortunate circumstance, he'd find himself squeezed between Fish Boy and a set of Siamese Twins and surmising that the twins wouldn't even be Siamese. Knowing the degree of shiftiness circus outfits were willing to employ to deceive the public, the girls would be Mediterraneans who, with proper clothes, makeup and lighting would be *passed off as* Siamese. They wouldn't even be conjoined, only well-trained to position themselves close enough to one another at all times to effect the illusion. Public expectation would fulfill the scenario, the saying, "clothes make the man," applying to these deceptive maidens as well as him. It was the pockets of his apparel that made him what he was, a very tall man with a lot on his mind and in his clothing.

Nicholas accepted his height like a soldier accepts his orders to the battlefront, a nun her association with God and a prisoner his last meal. But whereas the soldier, nun and prisoner could claim entrapment, the withholding of material facts or an outcome not of their doing, he realized justifying or denying his height would prove as big a folly as trying to park a hot-air balloon between two natural gas factories.

Doorways had to be ducked under. When riding in a motorcar he had to lean the seat as far back as possible, as if visiting the dentist, and when he tied his shoelaces he'd lift his foot instead of reach to the floor. The sudden altitude change made him dizzy.

Extraordinary height in his boyhood was a boon, towering over everyone on the playground and never needing to jostle to the front to see a parade. But his aerial advantage had drawbacks. Hiding in hide-and-go-seek proved impossible. When a fort got built, a tower had to be added for him.

By his early teens, all beds were too short. He remembered the day his class learned about "Honest Abe," Lincoln's feet sticking out wherever he slept. For the rest of that week his classmates referred to him as Stinkin' Lincoln. Friday's final bell took forever, like a turtle fleeing a burning house.

It wasn't in his nature to hold a toy, ball or schoolbook over another child's head and dare him to retrieve it, but throwing or catching a ball involved little chance of anyone's interference. Nicholas could reach any shelf and when it was time to paint or repair the house, he attended to everything above six feet without scaffold or assistance.

There was a phase where other children wanted to ride him like a giraffe, and in his attempt to fit in among his tender colleagues, he acquiesced. But the games took on a sadistic nature like drive-the-wild-monster-from-the-village, slay-the-giant or, his least favorite, that's-a-mighty-tree-but-it-must-come-down. In this last game, they'd strike his legs with sticks and bats as if he was a formidable oak whose time had come to be turned into boards and matchsticks. For most of his life, Nicholas felt he was being constantly chopped down.

"Nick-Old-Ass," as his teen peers christened him, came to enjoy walks alone in the forest, talking to the trees as if he were one of them, counting clouds or ripples in a body of water. By a stream, he'd wonder, *How much water has passed while I've been standing here?* and *How much has passed while I was thinking about it?* He'd tried poetry, most attempts fixated on questions of size and proportion rather than nature and romance.

Now a *very* tall *man*, Nicholas felt at the mercy of everything. Tax collectors, parking meter people and television programs were robbing him of what few pleasures he could find in a day.

Working as a kitchen-conveniences traveling salesman, Nicholas, nicknamed The Santa Salesman because he gave some goods away up front in order to not have the door slammed with a shriek, had his motel room burgled. He'd deposit all cash except enough for his meal in the motel safe before going out so he hadn't lost his or the company's money. Instead, what had been pilfered were his expensive, custom-sized suits.

The broadcast report of the theft fixated on his size, not the crime. People being what they are, rumors of a giant in the area circulated. To keep focus from him, Nicholas adopted a vagabond lifestyle, never staying anywhere more than a week.

It wasn't the media's and people's fabrications that bothered him. The stories he'd been writing and collecting in the suit pockets were gone. Even more distressing, his room was broken into next day, the rumpled suits returned.

He reached into the front pants-pockets of the first suit. Nestled in the cavernous fold was the short story he'd been writing before the theft. It was the same with the next suit and the next, each pocket containing one of the stories he'd been writing.

Until now, his exceptional elevation had been a scourge. His height made it impossible to be intimate, a gesture as simple as a kiss proving disastrous. Bending to do the deed was an aeronautical experience, like a jet fighter making a thousand-foot nose-dive, and pulling up at the last possible moment to plant the goods on target, so he made an uncertain peace with solitary life. That's when the stories began pouring out like a geyser.

Either he'd unconsciously placed the stories in his pockets or they appeared there on their own. Regardless, he was headed down a path of insanity. Like potatoes rooting in his trousers, stories sprouted in his pockets and could be harvested as needed.

Publishing under the *nom de plume* Charlie Quill, his books at first met with a modicum of success, and Nicholas/Charlie began dressing eccentrically so people would respect his privacy. It made him house-poor, spending all the royalties on his wardrobe, but wearing custom-made clothes, he achieved the reputation of being a writer who, like a magician with a rabbit in his hat, could literally pull a story out of a pocket. This increasingly surreal phenomenon affected his *condition*. Stories sprung up in his left pocket as well as his right, where they'd first appeared. To maintain his sanity, he labeled those in his left *raw manuscripts* and those in his right *ready for proofing*.

A rhythm emerged. Reaching in his coin pocket to retrieve *ideas*, he'd place them in his left pocket then transfer the manuscript to his right where they'd be polished for publication. If a story needed a twist, he'd reach in a back pocket. For something poignant, romantic, sentimental or humanistic he'd dip two fingers in his vest. Appearing helter-skelter in various stages of completion and Nicholas never knowing if they'd materialize, the process made him a slave to his muses. Like Van Gogh cutting off his ear, Nicholas Crockett aka Charlie Quill was ready to put a gun to his head.

Dozing one sleepless evening, the idea came to him that, if swift enough, he might leave his literary shackles behind by running into a clothing store, buying new suits and leaving the originals with instructions for them to be burned, recollecting how his childhood friends had tried to set him ablaze during a particularly frenzied game of 'what-a-mighty-tree'. Stories were in his new clothes. A welder's outfit, a suit of armor or a clown costume, they were with him for the long haul, and over the years they grayed his hair and wrinkled his skin so that a lengthy grooming ritual had to be added to his normal morning regimen. Dousing himself with expensive cologne, he hoped that, if fear was a tangible scent, the olfactory camouflage would keep anyone from detecting it. Having made a truce with his mysterious talent, a stalemate with his unnatural stature and meticulous daily preparations to insure his secret, one day he was found out.

Scrunched in a corner booth on the mezzanine of a

prestigious Copley Square hotel, nationally-acclaimed author Charlie Quill was spotted enjoying a fabulous, high-end, Beantown breakfast buffet.

That particular morning, gastronomically gratified and, as always, discreet to the point of being paralyzingly dysfunctional, Charlie Quill approached his luxury vehicle, oblivious that he was being followed.

Opening the door and climbing in, his stalker hissed, "Enjoy your breakfast?" Thinking it was a fan, Charlie nodded.

The stranger stared and Charlie wondered if this man might gun him down, Charlie having that thought about everyone he met.

In a canary-yellow silk jacket, powder-blue slacks, a pale orange shirt, gold neck chain, designer sunglasses and expensive Milano shoes, the stranger stood menacing, motionless and unspeaking. Thinking this the inspiration for a psychological thriller wherein the protagonist's life is in grave danger, Charlie wanted to reach in a pocket to find out, but not wanting to entice the stranger to go for something he might be hiding in *his* pocket, Charlie placed one hand on top of the open car door and the other on the roof of the vehicle, hoping by showing his hands that he meant the man no harm.

The instigator didn't speak. Charlie sighed.

"I asked if you enjoyed your breakfast?" the eccentric repeated, glancing left and right, assessing the surroundings, his body language suggesting he wasn't leaving before getting an answer, his question a sadistic command.

"Yes, I did," Charlie said with fear and obstinacy, the intruder slithering towards him and Charlie concluding this man wasn't an autograph hound, wanted *something* and might be on to Charlie's literary peculiarity. "Why do you ask?" Charlie wanted to get in his car and never return, finding some alternative activity that would satisfy his need for a daily half-hour of normality.

"I've been watching you," the peacock said, maneuvering to the front of Charlie's car. "You don't fit in."

"How do you mean?" Charlie asked, struck with the "chopping down" sensation he'd been fleeing his entire adult life.

"You keep reaching in your pockets, and each time, you get a strange look on your face."

"Really?" Fear oozed from Charlie's pores. He needed to know how far this man would go. The world of very tall man with very deep pockets' was in jeopardy again.

"It's as if you're playing with yourself and fighting the urge," the other man said, moving to the driver-side of the car.

Having forfeited flight as a viable option, Charlie's brain focused on the singular thought of personal preservation. Denied safety and comfort throughout his pre-author existence, he was adamant about keeping his life from becoming precarious again. Slamming the man with the car door and then running him down would bring police, media and more negative notoriety, the next to last thing he needed. The last thing he needed was this socio-pathic bastard to push him any further. In his final appeal, Charlie proposed what he believed a mediated settlement.

"How about I get in my car, drive away and never come back? Will that make you happy?"

"When I saw you in that corner booth messing around in your pockets I thought I was on to something. Now I'm positive."

"What do you think I'm up to?"

"You're hiding *something*."

A sprocket in Charlie's brain snapped, a plug came out, a switch flipped. He shook his head morosely, grimly, clenching his fists and lowering them to his sides like a gunslinger daring an outlaw to draw his firearm first.

"You think you know about me?" Charlie had never let anyone in on the secret of his stories. He reached into his left pants pocket. Whoever he was, this nosy shit clearly measured his happiness by the pain he caused others. The thought made Charlie cringe. Was it so much to demand a half hour each morning during which he could feel as if he were still a member of the human race? Still, he knew what he must do. "My pockets are unimaginably deep."

"You're stalling."

Charlie nodded like a mafia Don passing judgment on an underling, pulling his hand out of his right pocket and brandishing a completed manuscript.

"This is the story of a spider."

"What's the name of this story?" the man asked, returning Charlie's dare, not knowing that with those words, he'd sealed his fate.

"The Spider That Couldn't Stay in Its Web."

"That's an odd title."

"Too late to change it now," Charlie said, luring his prey in.

"Come on then," the stranger said, lifting one then the other foot as if stuck to the ground.

"Sometimes one spider will catch another."

"How's that?" the man asked, pre-occupied with the

tugging at the bottoms of his stylish, European shoes. His confident smile collapsed into a thin, anxious line, as if he urgently needed a men's room, his eyes moving from the manuscript to Charlie to his inappropriately-acting footwear.

"The second spider grabs the first and pulls it closer and closer into its web. The first spider, feels itself sinking, its strength zapped when the second drives a poison stinger into it." Charlie flicked his hand. The man cringed and clutched his thigh, his mouth frozen in terror. Eyes widening, knees buckling, he jerked in a crippling spasm.

Squeezing his hands as the debilitated antagonist sunk to his knees, Charlie said, "Dragging its kill into the middle of its web, the second spider wraps the first in a deadly veil, and the first spider is never seen or heard from again."

Like a puppet-master entangling the strings to suck the remaining motion out of a marionette, Charlie raised his hands like a sorcerer. The man twitched maniacally, then was gone.

Placing the manuscript in his right pocket, Charlie climbed into his car. He'd purchase a new outfit, flashy like the man who'd tried to do him in. Removing a pack of cigarettes from his coat pocket, he lit one and drew on the filter. Exhaling, he watched the smoke wisp out the window, disappearing as if it had never been. Turning the wheel and easing into traffic, he decided to take a road trip south along the coast, maybe to Key West. There was a story between here and there.

Chapter 12

The Theft of Szprotka (Sprot-kuh)

One spring day at Number Nineteen Piastow Bytomskich (Pee-*ah*-stoof Bih-*tom*-skee), Apartment Seven, Fourth Floor, Professor Skoczek (*Skoh*-chek) was preparing the teaching materials he'd need for today's lessons. A bachelor, he hadn't been spoiled by feminine coquetry. He was healthy, didn't smoke or partake of alcohol and felt his work teaching English gave him the added physical stature he might otherwise lack. His hair and moustache had grayed, but wearing them like a modern-day Mark Twain, he'd retained vigor and virility for a man in his forties. Taking pride in his appearance, he was always groomed and well-kept in public.

Standing at his desk, surveying the books and papers assembled in stacks, one hand on his hip, the other to his lips, he said, "Szprotka, (*Sprot*-kuh = *little fish*) have you seen my pencil bag?"

Szprotka was a young and slender cat, with

sunflower-orange eyes. Of the mixed-and-mottled alley-cat variety, she looked like a little Guernsey cow, mostly white with grey-black splotches. Lying on her back licking her paws and rubbing her face in the middle of the professor's desk, she turned her attention to him when he spoke.

"Szprotka, have you seen my pencil bag? It's green. About this long." Szprotka had a fondness for anything she could drag to the edge of his desk and drop to the floor. Jumping down, she would bat it about until it slid under the sofa or came to rest in an obscure corner of the apartment. It could be a pen, pencil, paper clip, button, scrap of scrunched paper, old battery, even some food, like a noodle. Szprotka rolled onto her side and continued licking her paw, washing her head and ignoring the professor.

"Szprotka, if you've dragged my pencil case someplace, please tell me where it is or bring it here."

Szprotka stopped washing and looked at Professor Skoczek. Standing, stretching, she came to him on silent paws, swishing her tail, squinting her eyes and licking her whiskers. She nuzzled her head in the cup of the professor's hand and, purring, moved her head side to side. The professor relented, scratching her ears, neck and forehead. Satisfied she had re-established their relationship, Szprotka slid the length of her body against the professor's hand and as she did her tail brushed aside a sheet of paper. There was the pencil case. Professor Skoczek picked it up.

"Szprotka, you smart, little kitty. You've detected the very thing I was looking for." The professor bent to rub his nose to hers then finished getting his books and papers in order. Szprotka snuggled in the middle of the desk and resumed cleaning her face.

The professor carried his empty breakfast-plate and half-full carrot-juice box into the kitchen, placed the plate in the sink and put the carrot juice in the refrigerator. Szprotka watched out of the corner of her eye, then jumped from the desk and walked into the kitchen to check her food bowls.

Professor Skoczek poured some water for her. Sniffing at it, Szprotka leaped to the kitchen window sill to spy on the pigeons fluttering on the building-roof gutter. Removing a milk carton from the refrigerator, the professor filled Szprotka's milk bowl. Holding up the carton, he called her like all cats are called in Poland, "Kee-cha, kee-cha."

Szprotka turned from the mesmerizing birds to inspect the object in Professor Skoczek's hand. Finding it to be a carton of milk, she pounced from the window sill to slurp dainty tonguefuls of the sweet liquid.

Striding into the bathroom, Professor Skoczek turned the cold-water handle on the white pedestal sink. Cupping his hands beneath the gurgling flow, he splashed his face and hair, running his fingers around his head and massaging his scalp from temples to forehead, then dried his face with a hand towel, picked up his hairbrush and combed his hair without looking in the mirror. Putting toothpaste on his new, green toothbrush, he brushed his teeth, careful not to forget the ones in the corners and remembering to scrub their back-sides. Szprotka came in and launched herself to the top of the washing machine, the professor acknowledging her as if awaiting her approval. Szprotka winked.

"Yes, my little dear. I always remember to brush my teeth. They're the only ones I have and I want to keep them as long as I can." Szprotka elongated herself up the front of his sweater-vest, placing her front paws on his shoulders in a gesture of affection and fidelity. Professor Skoczek rubbed his cheek against hers.

"I'm going into the living room. Would you like to join me?" he whispered.

Szprotka loosed herself, hopped down and followed the professor to his desk, rushing ahead to bound onto it and turning to face him.

Professor Skoczek donned his tweed blazer from his wooden desk chair, placing his mini-tape recorder, mobile phone and camera in his pockets and his beret on his head. Hoisting his carry-bag to his shoulder, he walked to the apartment door. Opening it, his *komorka* (kuh-*mor*-kuh = *mobile phone*) rang.

"Hello?"

"Professor Skoczek, you are teaching here today at six o'clock, yes?" It was Magda, the slim, young and lovely Incredible English Language School secretary.

"Indeed. I will be there, prepared to teach."

"See you later today." They hung up.

Right hand on the doorknob, keys in the other, he called to Szprotka, "I am going shopping, my little fish," and pulled the door shut, locking it behind him. On the next landing up, repairmen were working. He could hear them speaking through the open attic door. It was ten o'clock.

Professor Skoczek bounded down the stairs, nearly bowling Mrs. Kuszak (*Koo*-shahk) over. Mrs. Kuszak offered a "*Dzien dobry*" (Gin *daw*-bree = *Good day*), then asked about Szprotka. Her husband was a veterinarian. She fed the stray cats living in the abandoned building on Josef (*Yoh*-sef) Street.

Returning her salutation, the professor said, "She is

fine," and edged around her rotund personage, continuing down the stairs and out into the bright and promising morning air. Looking up to his open, fourth-floor window, he called to Szprotka, "Kee-cha, kee-cha," but she did not appear. *Napping or playing with something*, he thought. Adjusting his shoulder-bag, he contemplated the things he must get and headed towards the market.

At the corner, two convenience-store girls stood in a shop doorway, arms crossed, talking. The professor waved, offering a friendly, "Dzien dobry." They returned his greeting and asked about Szprotka.

"She is fine, thank you. And how are your cats?" he asked the closest girl.

"They are well," she said, "the best of friends."

Professor Skoczek walked down the middle of the street. Coming towards him was a young girl with blonde hair braided in dreadlocks, her Doberman Pinscher carrying a plastic bag in its mouth. Sometimes Professor Skoczek saw the girl riding her bike, the dog running behind. Sometimes he saw them walking with friends. Sometimes he saw her in the store on the corner, her dog sitting patiently out front. When he saw them by the fountain on the square, her Doberman would be lapping the fountain's spray. Professor Skoczek continued past the plumbing-fixture store, the butcher's and the baker's shops.

Down the street where the market began, women were hawking bouquets of bright flowers. Professor Skoczek thought how wonderful nature was to create such beauty. Turning into the bazaar, he noticed a *bezdomna* (bez-*dohm*-nuh = homeless woman), sitting at a low table aside the crowded entrance, puffing the stub of a previously-smoked cigarette. She had small dark eyes, thin grey hair and missing teeth. Two swollen legs showed from under her skirt. Shifting from foot to foot like an elephant trying to pound the earth beneath its massive feet, she was wearing a coat of lighter, newer, green material than her usual heavy, winter, brown one.

Saying, "Dzien dobry," he slipped a coin into her hand. She smiled, nodded and turned her attention to the other people entering and exiting the market, flicking the remainder of her cigarette stub into the street.

At the first stall, Professor Skoczek checked the prices of tomatoes, lettuce, green peppers, bananas, strawberries, onions, potatoes, spinach, grapefruits and apples. Passing the candy shop on the left and the meat shop on the right, a white-haired woman with a puckered smile was calling attention to the hand-embroidered clothes she had for sale. Noticing the professor, she gave his hand a squeeze, wishing him well, telling him her leg hurt today. Professor Skoczek returned the squeeze with a kindly nod.

Two shop girls working separate grocery stalls across from one another vied for his attention. He winked at each and they returned his familiarity. The maiden on his right wore a white frock with a bright blue flower pattern. She smiled, averting her eyes. The one on his left wore a blue frock embroidered with a woodland design. She smiled, holding his gaze. Professor Skoczek touched his beret and moved on with spring in his step.

At the far end of the marketplace, a narrow aisle turned to the right and became a conglomeration of second-hand shops with goods crammed onto rickety wooden tables. Shoppers browsed wares and haggled over prices, the din rising and subsiding as the professor wound through the knots of people engaged in hearty commerce.

Ahead, the market led into a side street, the Romany section where gypsy-ish sorts on both sides of the alleyway displayed goods at their feet or over their arms, backs against the buildings. Behind these hawkers, makeshift shops conjoined in a block-long facade mimicking the horseshoe-shaped cobblestone street barely wide enough to admit one car, much less two opposing ones. These shops sold alarm clocks, batteries, watches, straps for the watches, toenail clippers, scissors and wind-up toys. In the middle, to his left, behind a man showing off a sidewalk chalk-drawing was a modest-sized music shop. As if summoned by premonition, the statuesque, Venus-like shop-owner appeared in the doorway. Wearing a sheer blouse and jeans that outlined her hips and hugged her legs, she lengthened her torso and arms up the door-frame like a cat, her bronze, store-bought tan making her the most exotic woman in Bytom.

Wrenching his attention from the siren's hypnotic display, here at the end of the market were the best buys. At a vegetable and fruit stand overseen by an elderly, hump-backed woman, Professor Skoczek inspected the onions in her cart. Finding them to be the best value, he purchased four. Buying a kilo of potatoes, he waved and walked to the corner where a plump woman had bulbs of garlic and bottled mixtures for *zurek* (*shor*-ek = *sour soup*) on display. She was happy to receive payment for three bulbs of garlic and the professor was as pleased to put them in his shoulder bag with the onions and potatoes. Moving up the street, he procured a head of lettuce and a grapefruit from one stall, some strawberries, green peppers and bananas from another, tomatoes, spinach and apples from a large stall near the market entrance and some butter and grapefruit juice from the shop behind it. Arranging everything in his shoulder-bag, he started back the way he'd come.

A German Shepherd with her head and front paws hunched over a treasured chicken foot was crunching it loudly, engrossed in the rapture of the chew. He spoke to her, but she didn't look up.

On Josef Street he came to his familiar convenience store and went in.

"Dzien dobry," he said to the store-keeper and purchased six bread rolls, a five-liter bottle of water, some cheese, a carton of milk, a packet of macaroni and two boxes of carrot juice.

"How is Szprotka this morning?" the shop-woman asked. She and Professor Skoczek had found Szprotka crouched in the rain and shivering miserably in front of the store one night. Professor Skoczek had brought Szprotka to visit several times.

"She is well, most likely sleeping or playing with something from my desk."

"Give her a pet for me, will you?"

"I will."

The shop woman priced Professor Skoczek's items. He added them to his nearly-full shoulder-bag and stepped into the street again. An elderly woman, face hidden beneath a drab babushka (buh-*boosh*-kuh = a triangular scarf worn over the head) waddled by, a plastic bag hanging from each hand. Professor Skoczek handed her a coin as she passed and she thanked him, surprised he'd do such a thing.

At Number Nineteen Piastow Bytomskich, Professor Skoczek turned into the parking lot. Several men were standing and talking, drinking inexpensive, locally-made apple wine. They didn't look as he walked past. He stuck his key in his building door and turned it. Metal grating on metal, and the door sighed open.

Ascending the stairs he paused on the first landing to hear recorder music being played by the man in Apartment Number One. It filtered into the hallway like spring wildflowers spreading across a forest meadow. On the second landing Professor Skoczek smelled *zurek*, that intricate olfactory mix that enticed his nostrils and tempted his taste buds. The scintillating aroma stirred his culinary sensibilities, and he imagined himself standing over a cast-iron cook-pot, peering into it like a seer divining the future in a crystal ball. On the top landing, his neighbor's dog, Jacob (*Yuh*-kub), barked an alarm.

"Good dog, Jacob, good dog." The barking dampened to anxious whining, though Jacob continued scratching at the door. Professor Skoczek worked the key in his apartment door and stepped through the entranceway into his kitchen. Placing the shoulder bag on the table, he emptied its contents, putting everything except the milk in the refrigerator, positioning a plate of milk like a flower-vase in the middle of the kitchen table.

"Szprotka, my little potato dumpling, come get some milk," the professor said, pouring a glass for himself and setting it next to the carton. "Kee-cha, kee-cha, muh-*loot*-kuh" (*little love*).

He stepped into the back room where Szprotka liked to sleep on top of the *meubleszonka* (*meb*-luh-*shon*-kuh = a series of foreboding, floor-to-ceiling closets connected side-by-side for storing coats, clothes, blankets and china ware). She wasn't there. He walked into the living room. She wasn't there either. He stuck his head in the bathroom. No Szprotka.

"It's as if she's disappeared," he said, checking each room again, this time on all fours, searching under the furniture. Still no Szprotka. "Where can she be?" Sitting at his desk, he called for her then checked the hallway closet. She wasn't *anywhere* in the apartment. Professor Skoczek walked to the front door and opened it. "Szprotka. Kee-cha, kee-cha." She didn't come running. He listened for her cry and heard nothing. The workers upstairs were gone.

"I think my cat is missing," Professor Skoczek

announced to himself, walking into his apartment to his desk, thinking about Szprotka and the tasks he must finish before today's lessons.

"I'll go out," he said, thinking, *she'll be here when I return. Perhaps she's hiding someplace. She is an inquisitive creature doing something of interest. When her curiosity wanes, she'll reappear, like Houdini from a magic box,* the professor assured himself. *She's somewhere near and fine and will return in her own good cat-time.*

Professor Skoczek positioned his shoulder bag across his back, locked the door behind him and descended the four flights of stairs. Outside, he looked up at his window, calling to Szprotka, hoping to see her.

"No worries," he said, feigning unconcern, having left his glass of milk untouched on the table.

On Rynek (*Rih*-nek) Square, people were carrying bags, pushing baby strollers, walking alone or in groups. A child cried. Her mother stopped to soothe her. A shopkeeper cleaned her windows. A street vendor invited passersby to purchase a pretzel. An elderly man with a cane moved at a minimally-concerted pace. A middle-aged man swept the sidewalk while his wife stood in their doorway berating what sounded like his pre-condemned earthly existence. Two boys ran up the middle of the street, hooting and calling to one another.

Professor Skoczek's eyes roamed the length and breadth of the red-brick plaza. A sun as bold as Salome's dance had pushed people's coats open and their hats off. Scarves hung untied about bare necks and flowed from jacket pockets. Winter had yielded to an Upper Silesian spring.

In the center of the square a cloud of pigeons swooped about the town fountain like foot soldiers maneuvering on a battlefield as near-symphonically-decibeled water-plumes shot into the air and dove earthward like cannon balls crashing, the spray dispersed in the vernal breeze.

A man on a sputtering, orange motorbike with a bench attached length-wise to the front fender was transporting two singing children, one banging a tambourine, the other clacking rhythm sticks.

Professor Skoczek held the glass door of Empik (*Em*-peek) Newspaper and Magazine Shop open for two blushing girls. He browsed the magazines and examined picture frames, matching their sizes with photographs he'd taken, noting the features of the newest cameras and checking their costs, then turning his attention to the newspapers. Scanning the headlines of several national gazettes, he chose the local one. Folding it under his arm, he took it to the counter, smiled at the register girl, paid, placed it in his shoulder bag and left the shop, taking his place in the square's squirrelish liveliness again. People were sitting on benches or standing, talking. A police car inched up the pedestrian lane.

In the crowd, the professor saw his friend Agnieszka (*Ag*-nee-*esh*-kuh = *Agnes*). She didn't notice him until walking by and he called to her.

"Agnieszka, dzien dobry."

Agnieszka stopped, surprised.

"Good morning, Professor Skoczek. Nice to see you. Where are you going today?"

"Shopping." He pointed to his shoulder bag. "I've bought a newspaper."

"I see."

"And where are *you* off to?" he asked.

"To meet a friend for coffee. Would you care to join us?"

"Thank you, but I have some things to do before lessons this afternoon, and I must get a haircut today." Agnieszka was a hairdresser in the shop where Professor Skoczek got his hair cut.

"How is Szprotka?"

"She's fine, only this morning I seem to have misplaced her."

"How do you mean?"

"I saw her before I went out, but when I returned she was nowhere to be found."

"She's probably sleeping behind a chair somewhere."

"Probably, but it is strange. I've looked in every usual place and she's not in any of them." An unspoken fear gripped him. He pushed it from his mind. "She's probably somewhere right under my nose."

"Say 'hello' when you find her."

"I will." They parted, continuing on their way.

Twenty steps further, Professor Skoczek was in front of Rossman's, the town drugstore. He held the door open for a woman exiting with a baby in a stroller, a little boy toddling behind her, looking longingly a last time into the store then running to catch up with this mother. The baby was bundled in a blanket sporting little, sleeping cats. The baby's tiny arms floated at her sides, her fingers curling and uncurling in rhythm to her dreams.

Inside Rossman's, Professor Skoczek passed the toothbrushes, toothpastes, mouthwashes, shampoos and conditioners and headed to the far-right corner of the store where he picked up a large can of dog food. Szprotka enjoyed the beefy chunks as much as fishy cat food.

"What's good for the dog is good for the cat," Professor Skoczek said, "for the most part."

Next to the pet food was the camera-film pick-up/drop-off kiosk. Professor Skoczek inspected the rows of envelopes to see if there was a packet for him and if he knew any of the names on the others. When he found one that sounded familiar or a street he knew, he'd imagine the pictures inside. There being no film for him today, he took the dog food to the check-out register, mentioning it was for his cat. Placing the can in his shoulder-bag, he exited the shop. Five girls were sitting on the low wall that ran down this side of Rynek.

Past the corner of Ulica Bytomskych (Oo-*leets*-suh Bih-*tom*-skih = *Bytomskych Street*) and down Ulica Gliwicka (Oo-*leets*-suh Glih-*veets*-kuh = *Gliwice Street)*, he came to Plac Kosciusko, (Plats Koh-*shoo*-sko = *Kosciusko Place*), a row of cabs lined up nose-to-tail like hippopotami lumbering to a watering hole.

He strolled past Big Star Jeans, an electronics shop and a popular Polish restaurant with mixed-matched tables and chairs, but the best Polish food-for-the-money. The aromas reminded him of the smells in his apartment building. Closing his eyes, he imagined a big plate of *bigos* (*bee*-gohs = *a pork dish*) and *placek* (*plats*-ik =

potato pancakes).

At the intersection, he waited as a trolley screeched by, its cars wobbling like old men hurrying to get out of the rain. There was no rain today, only beautiful, spring sunshine. The professor crossed the square, passed Kentucky Fried Chicken and turned onto Ulica Sandowa (Oo-*leets*-suh San-*doh*-vuh = *Sandowa Street*). The hair salon was several shops up on the left. He looked at the trolley across the street, watching the people inside the tram-cars vying for seats or good hand-holds as the tram jerked to a start.

Karina, Agnieszka's friend and co-worker, was cutting a woman's hair. Seeing Professor Skoczek, she flashed a friendly smile in the mirror. Professor Skoczek pointed to his head. Karina motioned with a nod that he was next.

Sitting on a hair-drying chair, he picked up a magazine and thought about Szprotka. *Where could she have gone? Under the bed? Under the couch?* She *was* fond of hiding everything she could abscond from Professor Skoczek's desk and it was natural they'd roll under *something* as she batted them about until becoming irretrievably wedged somewhere. She'd crouch and peer beneath a piece of furniture in search of a misplaced or forgotten toy. Spotting it, she'd stick her paw under, reaching as far as she could to scoop it out. Professor Skoczek imagined her bapping an empty spool of thread, a bottle cap or a crinkle-necked straw. Once a week, Professor Skoczek moved the furniture and retrieved her toys, placing them in the middle of the living-room floor, watching her examine each until, making her selection, the game would begin again. Like a sultan's treasure, the toys would lie in a pile as one by one each disappeared.

"I'm ready for you," Karina announced, the shop bell tinkling as the coiffed lady before him exited, preening herself in the glass window-reflection. Professor Skoczek replaced the magazine, picked up his shoulder bag and walked to Karina's station, removing his gray, tweed blazer and sitting in her salon chair.

"It's nice to see you, Karina."

"How have you been, professor?"

"As well as can be expected." Karina picked up her scissors and comb.

"Is something wrong?" she asked.

"Nothing's *wrong*, only I find it difficult to say everything is fine, perfect or fantastic when generally *something* no matter how slight is out of place in one's life."

"Good point." Karina returned her attention to cutting his hair. "And how is Szprotka?"

"There's a girl that can truly say everything is fantastic. She eats, plays, sleeps and lives a care-free life, only I think I've misplaced her."

"How do you mean?" Karina paused to take in what the professor had said.

"I haven't seen her since this morning and can't find her in the apartment."

"Perhaps she's hidden herself for a morning nap?"

"That would be logical, but I feel she isn't there. Call it a cattish premonition. I will see when I return home."

"She's there somewhere." Karina assured him. "Classic?" meaning the haircut style.

"Yes, please."

Karina worked with scissors and comb then electric clippers to trim the professor's neck and sides, finishing with a straight razor to edge all around.

Professor Skoczek liked the cold sting of musk oil Karina smoothed on his neck. Applying a small amount of gel, she used a blower to give him a 'perfect' look. In less than twenty minutes Professor Skoczek had his haircut.

After inspecting his image in a hand-held mirror reflected in the larger wall-mirror at Katrina's station, he climbed out of the chair, bid Karina a good day, tipped her well, sharing departing comments with several waiting patrons. He swung out the front door with a new lightness, beaming at all he passed, twice catching his reflection in a store window.

"Only today shall I look this good. I'll sleep on it, wash and comb it myself without gel and it will look like it does every day," he said to his debonaire reflection.

Coming to his building, he climbed the four flights of stairs. Turning his front-door key in the locks, he expected Szprotka to be there.

She wasn't.

He set the can of dog food on the kitchen table next to the glass of milk and called her. When she didn't come, he walked into the living room, placing the newspaper on his desk.

"Szprotka may not be *here*, but she is *somewhere*." From room to room, he inventoried under and above the furniture, all her favorite places. A knock sounded at the door. Professor Skoczek opened it. It was his neighbor, the doctor, with Jacob by her side.

"I've brought scraps for Szprotka," the doctor said.

"Thank you, she'll enjoy them."

"Kee-cha, kee-cha," his neighbor called.

"She's not here right now."

"Gone out?"

"I don't know." This drew the doctor's curiosity.

"You mean you don't know where she is?"

"Something like that."

"Have you looked everywhere?"

"I believe so."

"Perhaps she's gotten out."

"Perhaps."

"Well, these are for her and I hope she turns up soon." She handed the professor a brown-papered, twine-tied bundle.

"Thank you very much, doctor. Be well, Jacob."

Professor Skoczek closed the door and carried the meat scraps to the refrigerator. He called for Szprotka. No answer.

Could she have gotten outside? I left the door open for a moment when Magda called. If Szprotka crept out, she'd be in the hall, mewing to come in. Unless... the professor paused, "...she's gotten out the front door," he ended aloud. Opening the kitchen window and leaning out as far as he could, Professor Skoczek scanned the courtyard.

"Kee-cha, kee-cha, Szprotka...kee-cha, kee-cha." He waited, watched, listened. *Yes, she must be outside, and she'll come back,* he thought, "...unless something's *happened* to her. Most likely nothing has. She's fine...out walking awhile, taking in the sights, bird-watching."

Pulling his head in, Professor Skoczek walked to his desk and sat, reviewing his lesson plans for the day. Opening the living room window, he searched the street. People and cars were moving about, but there were no cats to be seen. He sat at his desk again, leaving the window open. The sun was out, the air hypnotically warm. He read the paper, his thoughts returning to Szprotka.

"What if she's downstairs trying to get in? She's probably waiting right now. I should go."

Using the banister as counter-balance, he swung around the stair corners and plunked onto the ground-floor landing, thinking he heard Szprotka and racing to the door. A squeaky twist and a gentle heave, and it opened. There was the welcome mat, but no Szprotka.

"I should go look for her," he said with renewed determination, thinking he'd be out only a while. Szprotka would be scratching the ground, investigating a garbage can, nosing up to another cat or sitting under a car, watching the day go by. This very minute Szprotka could be on her way home, happy to see her professor coming up the street. She'd quicken her steps and run to his welcoming arms.

Professor Skoczek called and called. He looked

under the nearby cars, first those parked next to the curb then the ones in the parking lot. He checked the dumpsters in the courtyard. No Szprotka. Walking along the curb, the professor searched for any sign she'd been there. Mrs. Kuszak, the veterinarian's wife, came around the corner with her dog.

"Nice to see you, Mrs. Kuszak," the professor said. "I am looking for Szprotka."

"Did she get out?" She tugged her dog to stop his straining the leash.

"I'm not sure, but I think so."

"Well, she won't go far. You provide her a good home. Cats appreciate that."

"Let's hope it's true for Szprotka." Anxious to continue the walk, her dog strained the leash again. Mrs. Kuszak held her ground and kept him from pulling her forward. "Check the courtyard next over, the corner by the abandoned building. I feed the stray cats there. She might have wandered over to mingle."

"I will do that now," Professor Skoczek said.

"Let me know when you find her," Mrs. Kuszak answered.

"I will, Mrs. Kuszak," he said over his shoulder.

Professor Skoczek walked past the clothing booth owned by Mrs. Kwiatek (Kih-vee-*ah*-tek = *flower*). They smiled and exchanged 'dzien dobry's,' but Professor Skoczek's mind was on Szprotka and he didn't stop to talk.

In the next courtyard, Professor Skoczek knelt to peer through the iron-grated door in the brick wall surrounding the abandoned building. The wall blocked his view. From the sidewalk he saw a nubile black cat padding towards him. When the cat saw the professor, it froze, eying the human intruder. For several moments neither made a sound or movement, then Professor Skoczek spoke.

"Kee-cha, kee-cha, kitty. *Chodź tu* (*hoach*-too = c*ome here*)." The black cat was wary. It would not approach, staring at the professor as if he was a rare piece of art.

Professor Skoczek suspected this was one of the cats Mrs. Kuszak fed. The cat had come to see what there was to eat and the professor was standing where the cat wanted to be. Slowly, the professor side-stepped from the gated entrance and as he did so, the black stranger hunched.

"Kee-cha, kee-cha," the professor repeated, crouching and extending his hand. The cat leaped like a coiled spring, dashing through the gate to the security of the abandoned building.

A group of high school students rounded the corner on their way to the Gloria Movie Theater on Rynek Square. The girls giggled and nodded, tossing their hair and widening their eyes to emphasize amazement at what another had said, books strapped in their backpacks or clutched to their chests. The boys walked lazily, jostling one another, deliberating on the virtues and shortcomings of various *futbol* players.

"Hello, Professor Skoczek," one of the girls said.

Professor Skoczek searched the faces to recognize the speaker. He spotted the triplets, Agata, Beata and Renata (Uh-*gaw*-tuh, Bee-*aw*-tuh and Reh-*naw*-tuh), beautiful, long-limbed girls, each with waist-length chestnut-brown hair. Professor Skoczek couldn't tell them apart, always addressing them collectively as "you girls" or "young ladies."

Suspecting Professor Skoczek's dilemma, one of the triplets asked, "Who am I?"

Professor Skoczek concentrated then answered, "It's obvious you are you," and before they could taunt him further, added, "Nice to see you young ladies. Where are you off to?"

"The movies," Beata in the middle said.

"We're going with our class," Agata on the left said.

"It's an historical film," Renata on the right said.

"We don't like history," they said, pouting and wrinkling their noses.

As the class shuffled by, Professor Skoczek made an observation he believed would help identify each triplet singularly. Agata always stood to the left, Beata similarly in the middle and Renata constantly to the right.

"Why were you talking to that black cat?" Beata in the middle said.

"What did you say to make it run away?" Agata on the left asked.

"What were you looking for in that abandoned building?" Renata on the right wanted to know.

Answering Beata's question first, he said, "I wanted the black cat to come to me." Answering Agata's next, "I said, 'kee-cha, kee-cha, come here,' and it ran inside." Answering Beata's question last, "I've misplaced Szprotka. I thought she might be in this abandoned building. A number of cats seem to live here."

"Szprotka is missing?" the girls asked.

"I believe this is true. One doesn't like to ponder losing a cat; a purse, wallet, hat or even a car on occasion, but not a cat."

"Where do you think she is?" Beata in the middle asked.

"Could she have gotten far?" Agata on the left

inquired.

"Would you like us to help look for Szprotka?" Renata on the right said.

"I have no idea where she might be, but I don't think she could have gotten far. Aren't you girls on your way to see a film?"

"It's an historical film," Agata said, scrunching her nose.

"We don't like historical films," Beata said, scrunching her nose like Agata.

"It will be boring," Renata said, scrunching her nose like her sisters.

"History sucks," they said.

Professor Skoczek smiled, having taught them this American colloquialism.

"We want to help look for Szprotka," they said, like hummingbirds hovering at a sugar-water tube.

"You won't get in trouble skipping the movie? I could use your help."

"No and good," they said, laughing as they did.

"I'll look in the market," Beata in the middle giggled like a gurgling teapot. "Maybe Szprotka's gone shopping."

"I'll walk to Rynek and look there," Agata on the left snickered like a puppy wanting to play. "Perhaps she's chasing pigeons."

"I'll look at the tram stop at Plac Sobieski (Plats Soh-bee-*ess*-skee = *Sobieski Place*) and around the high school," Renata on the right, said, tittering like a pixie peeking out from under a forest leaf. "Perhaps Szprotka smelled the *kielbasa* (keel-*buss*-uh = *sausage*) there at the hot dog stand."

"Let's meet here in an hour and a half," Professor Skoczek said.

"Here in an hour and a half," the girls said, each going her way, spirits matching the promising day.

Professor Skoczek headed to Plac Kosciusko. Szprotka had to be somewhere in this city and with the help of the triplets he was going to find her.

At the market, Beata said, "If I was Szprotka, where would I go? *Not* in any abandoned building, too dirty, and no fun. I'd go see pretty flowers." Pleased with her cat-like reasoning, Beata hurried down the street, backpack bouncing side-to-side with each step.

Stopping in front of the largest flower stall, she scanned the ground, expecting to see Szprotka with her nose to some petals, enjoying the sweet aroma of colorful spring. Several women were bundling bouquets in one hand, tying them adeptly with a length of ribbon in the other. Bending to smell a clump of wildflowers, Beata savored their thick sweetness, forgetting her task until a stray cat slunk by and Szprotka popped back into her mind.

"Have you seen a little cat?" Beata asked one of the flower-women.

"What kind of cat?" the stall owner said, taking a moment from her tying to answer.

"A cat as sweet as your flowers. Her legs, belly and sides are white. Her tail, back and crown are gray. She's wearing a red and white collar. Did she come this way, perhaps to smell your flowers?"

The stall owner finished tying a bundle of bright blue, short-stemmed, forget-me-nots to a handful of pinkish-white, longer-stemmed daisies with a thin, yellow satin ribbon. Her hands moved instinctively as she thought, finishing the bow without looking at it.

"A big gray-and-white cat sits across the street in that doorway in the morning when I arrive. He sneaks off when things get busy, but no, I haven't seen a cat like yours." She thought again, to be sure, then slowly drew out her last words like a boat rubbing against its mooring. "Noooooo, I haven't seeeen that cat. Sorry, I can't help you."

"That's okay," Beata said, admiring the vibrant bouquet the woman held in front of her. "How much?"

The woman looked at it as if startled to find something in her hands. "Two *zlotych* (zih-*wah*-tee = *fifty cents*)."

Beata paid and continued down the street, holding the flowers to her nose, calling, "Szprotka, where are you?"

On Rynek Square, the town fountain was spouting its spindly fingers to the blue sky. Pigeons cooed and pecked at a toss of bread crumbs spread in a circle about an elderly couple's feet, their terrier sitting calmly between them. Straying too near the dog, flustered pigeons would fly off only to return to battle for better bread-crumb position. Some hovered mid-air in front of the couple, conflicted whether to land on an arm for more exclusive feeding or to join the multitude of feathered creatures on the ground. One landed on the man's hat. Realizing that wasn't where the action was, it descended to the gentleman's outstretched hand and pecked at a morsel held between his fingers. Without a command from man or woman, the terrier laid down, head on its paws.

Agata stopped in front of a woman selling sunglasses from a cart. Examining a rectangular pair with yellow lenses, she eyed oval ones with blue lenses and a heart-shaped, pink-lensed pair, thoughts of Szprotka having flown from her mind. She tried on the rectangular pair with yellow lenses and inspected them in the mirror, tilting her head left then right.

"Uh-*wuh*, I look like a movie star."

The sunglasses-seller was helping a man find a pair to suit his tastes and didn't acknowledge Agata's presence. Removing and placing the rectangular pair on the rack, Agata picked up the oval pair with blue lenses, put them on and searched the mirror as she had with the first pair, turning her head left and right.

"I look like a cool, jazz musician," she said, mimicking a saxophone-player, bending forward for the low notes and tilting her head back to wail on the higher ones. Looking at her reflection, she replaced them on the rack and picked up the heart-shaped pair with pink lenses. Peering into the mirror, she said, "Uh-*wuh*. I'm a country music singer," mouthing a plaintive, lost-my-lover song.

"Hello," the sunglasses-woman said. "Those glasses look absolutely *fabulous* on you."

Agata was about to say, "Yes, they do," when she remembered Szprotka.

"Have you seen a cute little cat come by today?"

"Cats come by here a lot, especially from back there in the courtyard. What does your cat look like?"

"Her legs, belly and sides are white. Her tail, back and crown are gray. She's wearing a red and white collar.

Did she come this way, perhaps to look at your sunglasses?"

"There was a tiger-striped cat, and a big, fat, mostly black one, but, no, I haven't seen *your* cat."

Agata said, "If you were a cat, where would you go?"

The sunglasses-woman scrunched her eyebrows, either because she was thinking or because the sun was in her eyes and she wasn't wearing sunglasses. Then she puffed out her cheeks, lowered her eyebrows and un-wrinkled her forehead. "If I was a cat in this town and it was a beautiful day like today, I'd sit by the fountain and watch the water spray into the air. That's what I would do."

"Yes," Agata said, wagging the heart-shaped pink sunglasses in her hand. "That's exactly what I'd do." Then she said, "How much for these?"

"Only three *zlotych* (zih-*wah*-tee = *seventy-five cents*), and they look *darling* on you."

"Yes, they do. I'll take them."

Agata paid for the sunglasses, thanked the woman for her advice and headed across the square, certain she'd find Szprotka sitting on the stone edge of the fountain. Her sunglasses gave everything a rose-colored tint. She'd be holding Szprotka in her arms soon, caressing and scolding her for having scared Professor Skoczek. Agata would explain to Szprotka how concerned the professor had been and maybe offer her a peek at the world through her new eye-wear.

Bounding up the stone stairs of Rynek Square, her Doc Martin Army Boots click-clacked on the cobblestone pavement. She'd had the shoe-man put metal cleats on the heels and toes so they wouldn't wear down as quickly and so she could tap-dance as she walked. She'd saved for several months to buy them. Someday she'd travel to New York City, learn to dance, and become a Broadway star. When she tired of the bright lights and glitter, she would return to Bytom and teach Dance. That was her dream and she lived it in that moment, dancing and leaping in circles, moving her arms like the ballerinas she'd seen in movies. The world went around in pink spins until she found herself next to the fountain. The spray from its fronds misted her face and hands, reminding her she was looking for Szprotka. Standing by the fountain, she looked left and right and breathed deep, not because the dancing had taken her breath, but because the air was moist and sweet with the smell of fresh-cut flowers. The combination of warm sun and cool spray felt so-o-o-o-o-o good.

Sitting on the lip of the fountain, Agata retrieved a

bag of cookies from her jacket pocket, removed one and held it to her mouth like a day-time full moon then took a bite.

With the sun on her face, she tapped the heels of her boots on the stones. Under the roaring fountain, savoring the oatmeal-and-raisin treat, she called, "Szprotka, where are you?" Her words drowned in the water's booming splashes as quickly as they were spoken.

On Plac Sikorski (Shih-*kor*-skee = *Sikorski Place*), Renata waited for traffic to stop on Ulica Katowicka (Kat-uh-*veets*-skuh = *Katowice Street*). A tram paused at the corner. It was one of the new French ones, clean, freshly painted a no-nonsense gray, unlike the old, rickety red ones that bounced passengers like lottery balls and screeched like giant prehistoric birds as they traveled to and from the provincial capital of Katowice (Kat-uh-*veets*-uh). Renata wondered why the town council had waited so long to purchase these new trams. The elderly had to be extra careful not to get knocked down by the heaving motion of the ancient, noisy beasts. They were freezing in winter and stiflingly hot in summer. Renata thought how shameful it was that politicians were more interested in stealing public money than using it for its rightful purposes of efficient public transportation and better salaries for workers, and for teachers as inspiring as Professor Skoczek.

Renata would begin law school in Warsaw next year, imagining entering politics and becoming Poland's first woman president. She'd make politicians see how much people were suffering. She'd thaw their frozen hearts, unclench their grubbing hands and allow Good to follow its natural course to the ones who really needed it.

The thought of waving to grateful crowds faded, leaving her staring into the eyes of an over-sized Ricky Martin poster plastered on the side of a screeching tram. She glanced to the right of Ricky Martin. There was a Christina Aguilera poster as big, both of them smiling at her with perfectly white teeth. On the other side of Ricky was a Jennifer Lopez poster of the same dimensions and graininess. The three made a compelling advertisement for buying their music on the Internet.

Recalling the American Dr. Seuss story she'd enjoyed reading as a child, she sang, "I would not buy them in a store or on the Internet. Furthermore, I would not buy them on a train nor in the sunshine or the rain."

Traffic halted, the tram passed and Renata crossed the street. On the corner there was a ticket booth, a doughnut-and-coffee stand and a stall with fruits and vegetables. Renata stopped in front of the last, eyeing the nectarines then looked down the length of the block, inspecting the sidewalk and the high school steps, where people were coming and going like migrating wildebeests. She scanned the boulevard for signs of a cat. The nectarines, her favorite fruit, caught her attention again. Renata ignored the temptation and walked up the sidewalk to the statue of Chopin. Surely a professor's cat would appreciate Chopin.

"Maybe Szprotka came to read the opera billboard," she thought out loud. The opera house was around the corner.

Renata checked the opera steps and the tram stands. At the corner, she peered up and down Ulica Moniuski (Oo-*leets*-uh Moh-nee*oosh*-kee = *Moniuski Street*). No sign of Szprotka. She crossed the street and walked down the other side, zig-zagging under the trees. There were lots of dogs, but no cats and definitely no Szprotka.

"Kee-cha, kee-cha," she called, looking in the trees as if Szprotka might be stranded in one. Renata had seen her climb the one in front of Saint Mary's on Rynek. Szprotka got a running start and bolted up its trunk. Coming to a branch, she stopped to look around. Szprotka wasn't in any of the trees.

At the next corner, Renata searched Ulica Katowicka (Oo-*leets*-uh Kat-uh-*veets*-kuh = Katowice Street). A thin, gray cat was slinking under some hedges.

Another cat was sitting on the cement wall, watching people pass. Renata walked to where the cat on the wall was perched. Lowering its head, ready to leap for safety, the cat stuck its nose out as Renata reached an open hand towards it.

"Kee-cha, kee-cha, *kota* (*koh*-tuh = *little cat*). Have you seen Szprotka? She has white legs, belly and sides. The rest of her, her tail, back and crown, is gray. She's wearing a red and white collar. Did she come this way, perhaps to buy a nectarine and take the tram to Katowice?"

The cat cocked its head. Backing away to let the cat consider her question in safety, Renata ran to the fruit and vegetable stand. Inspecting the nectarines, she bought the biggest, thinking how it resembled the morning sun coming up over the Mediterranean Sea, and a small jar of fish. Sprinting down the block, nectarine in one hand, jar of fish in the other, she stopped before the cement wall. Searching the sidewalk gutter, Renata found a discarded mini-pie tin. Turning the jar upside down, she gave it several good shakes and the fish plopped into the tin in one globby whoosh. When she set the tin on the wall, the cat's eyes widened. Reaching to pet it, the feral feline hissed, slicing the air in front of Renata's hand with its clawed paw.

"I must find Szprotka," Renata said, the cat's thoughts devoid of everything except the fish in front of it. Saying, "goodbye," she walked up the street, looking back to watch the cat eating. If she couldn't find Szprotka, at least she'd helped one of Szprotka's kind.

Professor Skoczek was standing at the corner on Plac Kosciuscko. He could see up Ulica Gliwice and across the square, but couldn't find Szprotka. She was someplace close. He could feel it.

Maybe she's napping under the bushes, he thought, looking at a line of shrubbery running halfway across the square to the memorial marking the division between the new and old part of town. The monument was an original block of stone left in place from the thousand-year-old town wall. A plaque placed in the ground sited the location of where the wall had once stood. What was left of the thousand-year-old battlement ran from there to Rynek Square and a block further. At that end, near Rynek, there was a stone tower where the infirmed and insane were left. Professor Skoczek's apartment building was within the boundaries of the old part of town.

Szprotka wasn't in the bushes.

Patrolling the perimeter of the square, he searched each side-street and passageway, circling past Pizza Hut and the courthouse, crossing and continuing to the next corner, turning right and coming back to Rynek where men were digging up the street, standing in a ditch to their waists. Picking at the hard soil, they tossed shovelfuls of dirt onto the sidewalk. Arriving at a narrow alleyway and recalling once having walked Szprotka there, the professor turned into it, thinking this is where she'd be.

At the far end of the passage, Professor Skoczek startled a black and white cat that poked its head out from under a garbage dumpster. The stranger looked at the professor then sprung over a retaining wall and disappeared. After glancing under the dumpster, he stood and turned completely around.

"Kee-cha, kee-cha, Szprotka. Come to me, little one. The triplets and I have been looking for you. Are you here?" He was running out of places to look. She was *somewhere*. He passed through a narrow walkway to Rynek, entering near a café with an excellent view of the entire square. He sat at a table under a large, outdoor umbrella, reflecting on the morning's events.

"Szprotka was *in* the apartment. I opened the door and answered my phone. She must have gone that moment. If she had gone to one of the neighbor's apartments, someone would have told me. If she's not in my apartment or anywhere in the building, where is she?

Someone could have let her out...or taken her. I don't think anyone would mean her harm, but it *is* possible. If she was let out, she's probably nearby and will return home soon, if one of us doesn't find her first." He thought about the triplets. "Perhaps one of the girls has her."

Across Rynek, he saw Agata bounding towards Piastow Bytomskich (Pee-*as*-stoof Bih-*tom*-skee) at the same time the waitress asked to take his order.

"Thank you, but it's later than I thought."

The waitress smiled and stepped sidewise as he stood. Professor Skoczek pushed his chair under the table and waved to Agata, calling her name.

"Agata." He noticed her pink, heart-shaped sunglasses.

She turned to the sound of her name.

"Professor, where are you coming from?"

"Plac Kosciusko (Plats Koh-*shoo*-koh)." He pointed over his shoulder in the direction he had come. "I thought Szprotka might be in the alley there. She wasn't, so I walked here to Rynek to sit and assess events thus far when I saw you. Are those new sunglasses?"

"Yes. I bought them there." She pointed across the square.

"They look very good on you. You haven't seen Szprotka have you?"

"No. I thought for certain she would be watching pigeons near the fountain, but she wasn't."

"It's time to meet with your sisters and review our findings. Let's catch them at the corner." They started down Piastow Bytomskich.

"Where do you think she is, Professor?"

"Just before I saw you and realized the time, I was thinking of how Szprotka came to be missing. I opened the front door. The phone rang. I hung up and went out. When I returned, she was gone. I've looked all over the apartment, in the closets and under the furniture. I'm certain she's not there. How she got out, or worse, whether she's been taken, I don't know."

"You don't think *that* could happen, someone taking her?"

"As I grow older, I've come to believe anything can happen, and if it can, it most likely will. A person wants to say, 'everything is going to be okay,' but usually, it isn't."

They were almost to the corner when the professor spotted Beata coming down the street on the left and Agata saw Renata coming towards them down the street on the right. Assembling at the intersection and no one having Szprotka, Professor Skoczek broke the silence.

"Those are lovely flowers, Beata. Did you get them

at the market?"

"Yes." She held them out for everyone to smell.

"Where did you get those hideous sunglasses?" Renata asked Agata.

Agata raised her chin. "I bought them on Rynek. I think they look good on me, don't you?"

"I *think,* alright. I *think* they look gaudy," Renata said.

"Then you won't want to borrow them like you do my other things."

"Hardly." Then Renata said, "Did anyone find Szprotka?"

No one spoke.

"Don't fret, girls," Professor Skoczek said. "Szprotka is close. The only question is where?"

"We can check the park on our way home," Beata said.

"That will be helpful," Professor Skoczek said. "Perhaps we should meet tomorrow morning?"

"Good idea," the three chorused.

"Let's meet at my apartment at a quarter to eight," the professor instructed.

"We should be getting back to school," Beata said. "Here comes our class." Down the street from Rynek Square their classmates were returning from the film. The triplets stepped into the corner store then into line when half the students had passed, winking and smiling at the professor. Agata pointed to her watch. *Quarter to eight. See you then*, she mouthed.

Professor Skoczek spent the remainder of the afternoon looking for Szprotka. When he saw some of his language students, he asked, "Where are you off to?"

"Your English class five minutes from now," one of them said.

Professor Skoczek jetted in the direction of his apartment building. "I will see you there, on time," he shouted over his shoulder, sailing down his street to his apartment. Putting on his sport coat and slinging his shoulder bag around his neck, he had three and a half minutes to get to The Incredible English Language School before the class bell.

Adjusting his beret like an aviator preparing for take-off, he filled his lungs with flowery spring air and launched himself down his building stairs then around the corner and up the street towards the square, adjusting his forward trajectory to enable a man on a bicycle to pass safely.

Whizzing by and puffing an apology, Professor Skoczek launched up Rynek's stone steps two at a time, soaring through a flock of pigeons scrounging crumbs on the brick pavement. Feathers flailing in a rush of flapping and cooing, the air reverberated with their frenzied confusion. Remembering the sack of breadcrumbs in his pocket, he exhumed the bag, raised it to his mouth, ripped it open with his teeth and, holding the bag above his head, flung the crumbs behind him as he dashed for class. Sensing the situation had turned from bad to good, the pigeons regrouped and swooped to the pavement for the unexpected windfall.

Professor Skoczek would have preferred to sit surrounded by appreciative birds, but there wasn't time for that, or to think about Szprotka. Flying down Ulica Strazacka (Struh-*zahts*-kuh = *Fireman Street*) and landing in front of The Incredible English Language School, he pushed open the heavy, wooden doors, whisked the beret from his head and scrambled up the three flights of stairs, past the director's office to his classroom where his teenage students were talking and joking. Regaining his composure, he stepped through the door, the raucous classroom calming to a respectful hush with the exception of one student, a boy named Przemyk (Pih-*shem*-mik). Brushing the sweat from his brow with the back of his hand, Professor Skoczek placed his satchel on his desk.

Przemyk was standing, his back to the door, left hand above his head, holding a wad of paper, his target, a girl named Maja (*My*-yuh = *Maya*) seated across from him. Przemyk knew someone had entered the room and from the sudden silence, that it was probably someone important. All eyes fixed behind him, Przemyk was ninety-nine percent certain it was Professor Skoczek, so he lowered his arm and sat, turning to face his professor.

Professor Skoczek closed the door and walked towards Przemyk. Everyone looked at one another guiltily. Przemyk's hands were on his lap, eyes lowered, lips closed tight. Standing behind Przemyk's chair, Professor Skoczek leaned forward.

"Good afternoon, class," Professor Skoczek said.

"Good afternoon, Professor Skoczek," the students said in unison.

"And good afternoon to you, Przemyk."

"Good afternoon, Professor Skoczek."

"Nice to see you in class today, Przemyk."

"It's nice to be in class today."

"I'm going to ask you a question and I want you to tell your classmates what the verb tense of the question is."

"Okay."

"This is the question. 'What were you doing just now'?" Professor Skoczek repeated it, "'What were you doing just now'?" and returned to his desk, leaving

Przemyk and his classmates to answer the question.

"Don't tell him the answer. I will repeat the question: What is the verb tense in the sentence, 'What were you doing just now'?" Professor Skoczek removed his coat and sat. Przemyk considered the possible responses, knowing only one could be correct.

"Say the question out loud so you can hear it."

Przemyk repeated, "'What were you doing just now'?"

"That is the question. Now, what is the verb tense?" Przemyk didn't say anything. Professor Skoczek assisted. "Is the sentence, 'What were you doing just now?' a statement or a question?" Przemyk's mental efforts were rewarded.

"The sentence, 'What were you doing just now?' is a question." Przemyk inhaled and exhaled in equally robust fashion.

"Good. Now, what is the verb tense?"

Przemyk thought out loud. "Were doing…were doing…'were' is the past tense of the word 'are'…the plural form of the verb 'to be'. 'Doing' is the present participle of the infinitive verb 'to do'. 'Be' plus 'ing'…in the sentence, 'What were you doing just now,' the verb tense is past continuous."

Everyone stared at Professor Skoczek, being careful

not to let his or her expression reveal the answer, each student considering carefully whether it was the same as Przemyk's. Giving no indication whether Przemyk's was correct, Professor Skoczek walked to the window, staring at the trees moving with the breeze. The class fidgeted. Some began to wonder if their professor knew the answer to his question. Professor Skoczek was thinking about Szprotka.

"Przemyk, in the sentence, 'What were you doing just now?' you said the verb tense was past continuous because 'were' is the past tense of the word 'are,' the plural form of the verb 'to be' and 'i-n-g' is the present participle form of the verb 'to do'." Przemyk considered the professor's summary.

"Yes, something like that."

"Something like that or that exactly?"

"That exactly. That is what I said, or what I meant to say." The class was perplexed.

Professor Skoczek asked, "Is Przemyk correct?" No one answered. "Maja?" (*My*-yuh = Maya)

Maja wished for all the world Professor Skoczek had chosen *anyone* other than her.

"Przemyk is *correct*?" Maja's rising inflection at the end of her sentence made her statement a question.

"Are you *sure* Przemyk is correct? Your answer

sounds like a question."

"I am *sure* Przemyk is correct."

"Good. Always answer a question with a statement. Lower your voice at the end of your answer. It makes you sound confident, and besides learning English, I want you to be certain of yourselves."

Przemyk's friend, Michał, (*Mee*-how = Michael) said, "Przemyk is correct," and everyone agreed.

"So, everyone thinks Przemyk's answer is correct." Professor Skoczek was looking out the window again. Anticipating the moment of truth, the class squirmed as Professor Skoczek released his thoughts of Szprotka, waited one moment more then said, "Przemyk *is* correct."

Everyone burst into applause, congratulating one another. Michał slapped Przemyk on the back and shook his hand.

"I knew you knew the answer. That's why I sit next to you for tests." The class laughed.

"Very good, Przemyk. Now, can you answer this question as easily as the first?" Przemyk smiled, nodding confidently and giving his classmates two thumbs up. Flush with success, everyone readied for the question. "Answer this for the class. 'What were you doing just now'?" Smiles faded.

"Professor Skoczek, I answered that question."

"You told the class what the verb tense of the sentence was. Now tell us *what* you were doing." Przemyk's face soured as if he'd been sentenced to death for some heinous indiscretion he was determined to take to his grave. Silence hung like Baltic fog as Professor Skoczek circled the classroom. "Let's make predictions about what Przemyk was doing when I entered. What is a prediction, Jacek (*Yuh*-sik = *Jack)*?"

"When you guess what happened, like a detective, or when you say what the future will be, like a fortune teller."

"Correct. Everybody, take a minute and think about what Przemyk *could have been doing* when I opened the door and Przemyk was standing with his arm above his head." Professor Skoczek turned to the blackboard and wrote: *'To make' a prediction. What was Przemyk doing? What could Przemyk have been doing?'*

Even with his back to the class, Professor Skoczek knew his students were glaring at Przemyk and Maja. Turning to the class, everyone's face became a mock-expression of serious thinking, some holding one palm to a temple, others with pencils to the corners of their mouths or suspended in the air as if they were poised at the edge of an epiphany...except for Maja. Her face was red. Przemyk slunk in his chair, groaning, wishing he could vanish unnoticed under the classroom door.

"Przemyk, are you ill?"

"No, Professor Skoczek, only a little uncomfortable."

"Relax. Everyone take another minute to think of a..." their professor paused and the class said, "Prediction." Professor Skoczek pivoted to the blackboard like an owl rotating its head and wrote: *Pzremyk could have been…__ing__*. Finished, he turned to confront his class.

"Okay," Professor Skoczek said, pointing to the blackboard. "Przemyk could have been 'verb plus i-n-g,' then the rest of the sentence describing whatever it was he was doing. Who would like to begin? Ania (*Ahn*-yuh = *Anna*)?"

"Can you repeat that, Professor Skoczek?" Ania asked, squinting at what the professor had written on the board.

"Przemyk could have been 'verb plus i-n-g,' then the rest of the sentence describing what he *could have been* doing."

"Thank you, Professor," Ania said. "Przemyk could have been pretending he was the Statue of Liberty in New York City."

"And what is the Statue of Liberty? Szimon (*Shee-*

moan = *Simon*)?"

"A lady in a long robe standing in the New York City harbor, wearing a crown and holding a book and torch."

"Correct. Szimon."

"Is she standing near the World Trade Towers?"" Marcin (*Mar*-cheen = Martin) asked.

"The Towers are on Manhattan Island, at Liberty and Church Streets. The Statue of Liberty is to the south and a bit east, on Ellis Island. What else could Przemyk have been doing?"

"He could have been signaling for an airliner to land," Edyta (Eh-*deet*-uh) said, "Like the man who stands on the runway wearing an orange vest, holding flags or flashlights."

"That's what I was doing," Przemyk said. "signaling an airliner."

"We shall see," Professor Skoczek said. "Mateusz (Mah-*tay*-oosh = *Matthew*), what could Przemyk have been doing?"

"I think the same as Szimon. Przemyk could have been signaling an airliner."

"That's what I was doing," Przemyk said with finality, looking from student to student for support.

"Mateusz," Professor Skoczek said. "Think of

something *else* Przemyk could have been doing. Use your imagination."

"Przemyk *could have been* holding hands with a giant." Everyone laughed, Professor Skoczek so hard he had tears in his eyes.

"What does this giant I was holding hands with look like?" Przemyk asked, grateful the conversation had taken a more comical direction and much lighter tone, delaying the embarrassment and reprimand he was fairly certain was very soon coming.

"He's twenty feet tall, has long red hair, one blue eye in the center of his forehead and only one big, crooked tooth in his mouth," Mateusz said, adding, "in front, on top, in the middle."

"Thank you," Przemyk said. "Now I will know him when I see him."

"That is wonderful," Professor Skoczek said. "Someone else. Wioleta (Vee-oh-*let*-uh = *Violet*)?"

"I can't beat that one, professor," Wioleta said.

"Try."

"Przemyk *could have been* Adam Małisz (*Mah-*wish) holding up the First Place Gold Trophy for Long Distance Ski Jumping."

"*Yes,*" the boys yelled, slapping 'high-fives'.

"Possible. Very possible," Professor Skoczek said,

staring across the rooftops. "One more before we move on. What could Przemyk have been doing, Claudine?"

Maja's friend, Claudine, said, "Przemyk could have been stretching his arm."

"Did his arm need stretching?" Professor Skoczek said, clasping his hands behind his back.

"He could have been bowling or dribbling a basketball and his arm got tired."

"That's what I was doing," Przemyk said. "I was playing basketball or bowling before class and my arm needed stretching."

Professor Skoczek said, "So, Przemyk, what *were* you doing? Stretching your arm, holding hands with a giant, signaling an airplane, being the Statue of Liberty… or something else?"

"When?" Przemyk said, pretending not to understand the question.

"When I came in and you had your arm in the air."

"Oh, that? That was nothing."

"If it was nothing, why were you doing it?"

"I don't know."

"Maybe you were doing something?"

"Maybe."

"Perhaps you had something in your hand?"

"I forget."

"Perhaps it was a paper wad and you were going to throw it?"

"It's possible."

"Is there a chance you were going to throw that paper wad *at* someone?"

"Now that you mention it, professor, it *is* a possibility." Przemyk smiled nervously.

Professor Skoczek moved to the rear of the class, stopped and leaned forward, placing one hand on Paweł's desk (*Puh*-vel = *Paul*) and the other on Joanna's (Yoh-*awn*-nuh = *Joanna*), his eyes going once around the classroom, everyone lowering theirs. Maja looked like she'd seen a vampire, Przemyk like a king whose empire had crumbled.

"It isn't a good idea to throw things in my class," Professor Skoczek said, "for two reasons. First, you might hurt someone. That is the best reason not to throw things in my class." Everyone nodded silent agreement. "The other reason is that if someone is injured in my class, *I* will be responsible. So please don't throw things in my class. May we all agree on that and remember it for the rest of the year? If you need to throw something at someone here at the Incredible English Language School, please do it somewhere other than in my class."

"Yes," the class chimed. "If we need to throw

something at someone here at the Incredible English Language School, we will do it somewhere other than in Professor Skoczek's class," their relief evident from the rising tone of their collective voices.

"Good. Any questions?"

Maja spoke. "How did you know what Przemyk was doing, professor?" Professor Skoczek returned to the front of classroom.

"As unbelievable as it may seem, I was a teenager once," he said.

Everyone strained to picture their professor as an adolescent.

"Any other questions?"

"How is Szprotka?" Michał asked.

Professor Skoczek sat at his desk and spread his hands in front of him. "Interesting you should ask."

"Why is that interesting, professor? We always ask about Szprotka."

"Yes, Michał, but your question is particularly interesting today because I cannot say how Szprotka is."

"Why can't you say how Szprotka is?" Krzysztof said (*Kshih*-stoff = *Christopher*).

"Is it because you don't *know* how she is?" Claudine asked.

"That is part of the reason."

"What's the other part?" Przemyk wondered out loud for everyone.

"I cannot say *how* Szprotka is..." Professor Skoczek hesitated, listening to his own astonishment, "...because I cannot say *where* Szprotka is. I don't know where she has gone."

"Let me get this straight," Michał said. "You don't know *how* Szprotka is because you don't know *where* she is."

"Correct."

"Szprotka is missing?" Paweł (*Puh*-vel) half-asked, half-stated.

"That is what I believe," Professor Skoczek said.

"Has she been cat-napped by pirates?" Szimon asked. Ania nudged his arm and he winced.

"I don't think her disappearance is as dramatic as that, but there *is* an element of mystery. What does the word 'mystery' mean?"

"Something is spooky or strange," Ania volunteered.

"Something you can't say why it is," Maja added.

"Mateusz," Przemyk said, mimicking Professor Skoczek. "Give us an example of *mystery* in a sentence."

Mateusz thought. "Sometimes, the English language is a mystery to me."

Everyone laughed, including Professor Skoczek. Mateusz squirmed with pleasure at his clever use of English.

"We should go look for Szprotka now," Przemyk said, standing and closing his workbook.

"Thank you for your enthusiasm, Przemyk, but we don't need to skip our English lesson to find her."

Przemyk flashed a puckish grin. "It's nothing," he said, sitting.

"I will look for her after school this evening," Professor Skoczek continued, "and will undoubtedly find her then. She can't be far away."

"We can all look for her with you," Monika (*Moh-nee-kuh* = *Monica*) offered.

"Thank you, Monika, but first, you will probably want to go straight home and do the English homework assignment I am about to give you."

The entire class moaned, their faces twisting into expressions of agony.

Professor Skoczek smiled. "Can anyone say where Szprotka could be? Izabela (Ee-zuh-*bell*-uh = *Isabella*)?" The shyest of Professor Skoczek's students, Izabela avoided speaking in class. Shaking her head from side to side, she pursed her lips. "Where do you think she could be?" Professor Skoczek asked again, drawing her out.

Izabela shrugged, raised her eyebrows and shifted in her seat. Professor Skoczek stood, went to her and crouched beside her desk. Looking at Professor Skoczek, Izabela forgot about her classmates.

"Maybe Szprotka is at home?" She lowered her eyes.

"If Szprotka is home, why don't I know where she is?"

Izabela crossed her ankles and folded her arms. "Maybe you can't see her," she whispered.

"Do you mean my brain and eyes are failing?" Everyone, including Izabela, laughed, then her expression intensified.

"No, Professor, that's not what I mean."

"Then what *do* you mean?" Michał challenged.

"What I mean is, Szprotka could be someplace you can't see her."

"You mean hiding somewhere?" Lucja (*Loots*-yuh = *Lucy*) questioned.

"Yes," Izabela said emphatically.

"Like in a closet?" Paweł asked.

"Maybe," Izabela said, "or perhaps *in* the couch."

"Did you say *in* the couch?" Szimon asked, "I have seen my dog *on* our couch, but I have never seen her *in* our couch."

"That's because you can't see a dog *in* a couch," Przemyk said.

"And you can't see a cat *in* a couch either," Izabela explained.

"Please continue," Professor Skoczek said.

"Once, our cat crawled *under* and up *in* the couch."

"I see," Monika said.

"But you still *can't* see a cat or a dog *in* a couch," Przemyk said.

"So when I go home this evening, I should look *under* the couch," Professor Skoczek said, bending and looking under his desk, "then up *in* the couch?" The class leaned under their desks as if looking up into Professor Skoczek's couch.

"That is what I would do," Izabela said, upside down like everyone else.

"An excellent idea," Professor Skoczek said, straightening. "Where else could she be?" Everyone raised their heads from under their desks.

"Well," Paweł said, "if she got outside, she could be anywhere. She could have gone down the street that way," he said, pointing to the left. "Or, she could have gone down the street the other way," pointing to the right.

"Does Szprotka have any enemies, someone in the building that doesn't like cats?" Szimon asked.

"None I know of," Professor Skoczek said.

"Szprotka could have been cat-napped by pirates," Szimon said. Both Ania and Maja gave him elbow jabs.

"Ouch." Szimon hunched his shoulders and rubbed his arms.

"That's for mentioning 'pirates' again," Ania said.

"Say 'pirates' one more time and see what happens," Maja added.

"Okay," Michał said, giving both girls sideways glances. "He won't say 'pirates' anymore."

"Yes, that's enough about 'pirates' for one class. Your homework for Thursday is…" everyone groaned and closed their books, "to write three paragraphs about where Szprotka *could be*," Professor Skoczek said, writing on the board. "In the first paragraph, tell why you think Szprotka is missing. *Szprotka is missing because...* In the second paragraph, list three places Szprotka could be. *Szprotka could be...* In the third paragraph, choose the place where you think she *most likely is* and give several reasons why you think she is there. *Szprotka is...place...because...*

"How many is 'several'?" Claudine asked, writing the notes for the assignment.

"More than 'two,' less than 'five'," Przemyk said as he sped out the door past her.

"That is correct. See you Wednesday. Everyone be well, do your homework and have fun." Several students groaned on cue at the word *homework*, their moans dissolving into the general enthusiasm of class having ended.

Claudine, the last student to leave, whispered with empathy, "I hope you find Szprotka." The classroom door whooshed closed behind her, muffled exclamations drifting down the stairwell and out of the building into the evening.

One student, which one he couldn't be certain, said, "The Theft of Szprotka." Standing alone, marking pencil in hand, he listened to the silence as the words filled him with dread.

Is Szprotka really gone? Could someone have stolen her? Packing his satchel, turning off the lights and making his way to the downstairs landing, he listened to his footsteps echoing on the wooden stairs, then walked up Ulica Strazacka to Rynek.

The moon cast an opulent sheen on the rooftops. Wispy clouds raced across the evening sky like sailboats on the Wisła (*Veese*-wah) River. Professor Skoczek stood in the center of the square. Gazing at the swirls of light circling like a dark version of Van Gogh's *Starry Night*, he said, "Szprotka, please come home." Opening his eyes, he sighed and walked to the corner convenience store where he purchased cheese, two tins of fish, a jar of pickles and a packet of cookies.

"How are you tonight, professor?" the shop girl asked.

"Fine, Joanna (Yoh-*awn*-nuh = Joanna), thank you. And you?"

"I still work here, but I am looking forward to finishing my last year of study. Then I will move someplace with a better economy and more opportunities."

"Yes, it is a shame."

"How is Szprotka?"

Instead of saying, "Szprotka is missing," Professor Skoczek said, "I'm sure she's fine," hesitating a moment before adding, "somewhere," this last word emptying out of him like air from a street musician's accordion. Joanna didn't notice. "See you tomorrow, Joanna."

"See you tomorrow, Professor."

Professor Skoczek crossed the street, feeling defeated. Two dogs tussling one another stopped to sniff him as he passed. Turning into his building lot, he found his keys. Holding his groceries in his left arm, he unlocked the outside door and climbed the stairs.

"Szprotka, when I open this door, you will be there,

happy to see me and home safe where you belong, no matter where you were," He recited like a Buddhist mantra. The locks clicked. Pushing the door, it swished softly. In the dim light no cat was waiting. "Maybe she's sleeping on the day-bed," he said, as if it would summon her like a genie from a lamp.

Professor Skoczek plunked the grocery bag on the floor and hurried to the living room, opening the clothes dresser and checking its shelves. He looked in the backroom closet and even under the bathtub. She'd never been away so long. She *was* gone whether he wanted to believe it or not. Numb and deflated, he returned to the hallway.

His cell phone rang. Pressing the talk button, he held it to his ear.

"Dobry wieczor," (*Doh*-brih vee-*etch*-or = Good evening).

"Professor Skoczek, good evening." He recognized the voice, his friend, Doctor Lighthouse. "Professor, good evening. We are going for a walk presently, and realizing your classes were finished, thought to ask if you might like to join us."

"Doctor Lighthouse, it is good to hear your voice. I've just now come from the Incredible English Language School and while I have something weighing on my mind, I'd be delighted."

"Excellent. It is a warm night and Piwo (*Pee*-voh = *beer*) is in the mood for a stroll in the park." Piwo was Doctor Lighthouse's Rottweiler, named 'Piwo' because he liked beer.

"Where shall we meet?"

"Do you know Café Irlandia (Ear-*land*-dee-uh = *Ireland Cafe*) on Ulica Biała (Bee-*ow*-wuh = *White Street*)?"

"I do. Shall we meet there in, say, twenty minutes?"

"That will be perfect. Piwo and I will be seeing you shortly."

"Perhaps you can help with a problem I have acquired."

"If I can be of service, I will be happy to assist."

"Your intuitions in matters of unexplainable occurrences will be appreciated."

"A bit of telepathy. All the better."

"See you soon, Doctor."

"Yes, Professor."

Professor Skoczek slipped his komorka into his pocket. Lugging the groceries into the kitchen, everything went into the refrigerator except the fish.

He looked at the can, and the word *Szprot* (Sprot) on the label. This was how Szprotka had gotten her name, *little fish.* Setting it on the table, he lifted the box of milk from its shelf in the refrigerator and poured some into Szprotka's bowl. The glass he'd poured for himself earlier in the day sat untouched.

Dark, skeletal clouds danced across the moon.

Placing the milk carton in the refrigerator, he grabbed a bottle of Farmer Jan's Sure-Good Carrot Juice, walked to his desk in the living room and sat, sipping in silence.

"If I was Szprotka, where *would* I have gone?" he asked, answering, "If I was Szprotka, I *wouldn't* have gone!" The carrot juice made him feel as if he was in the Cake and Ice Cream Mountains, a place he enjoyed taking Szprotka, near the Czech Republic border. They would dine on potato pancakes and beer, then walk up a cobblestone street and sit in a café for ice cream and a pastry. He closed his eyes and imagined them on a mountain path, Professor Skoczek picking blueberries as Szprotka lazed in the cool shade, batting and chasing the occasional blueberry that dropped to the ground.

Szprotka liked carrot juice as much as Professor Skoczek. He would pour some in the bottle cap and she'd lap the orange nectar, then lick her whiskers and paw his hand, asking him for more. There was no Szprotka tonight. He opened his eyes and leaned forward.

"Szprotka is *in this town* and I *will find* her." Replacing the carrot juice in the refrigerator, he put on his coat and descended four flights, stepping into the wavering moonlight and listening. Looking under dumpsters and hedges, '*kee*-cha-ing' as he went, he spied a sitting figure in the shadows leaning against a tree. His snoring sounded like a small gasoline engine was powering his dreams, his fingers rhythmically curling and uncurling around an empty wine bottle.

Searching and calling, the professor came to Ulica Poczta (Oo-*leets*-uh *Poach*-tuh = *Post Office Street*) and waited for the traffic light. When he could wait no longer, he crossed.

"You're supposed to wait for the light to change," an elderly woman scolded.

A block down, in front of Café Irlandia on Ulica Sąd (Sond = *Court Street*), Doctor Lighthouse and Piwo were waiting. Piwo snuffled and snorted as Professor Skoczek approached.

"Good evening, Doctor Lighthouse." Professor Skoczek patted and stroked Piwo and the Doberman wiggled his body and licked Professor Skoczek's hand.

"Piwo is a lover, isn't he, professor? Shall we walk?"

"This way, if you don't mind, Doctor, towards

Rynek. I'd like to have a look around there this evening." Piwo wanted to cross to the park. Doctor Lighthouse urged him down the sidewalk.

"What problem have you acquired, professor and how can my extra-sensory perceptions be of assistance?"

"I say this with some reticence, Doctor, but I have misplaced Szprotka."

"Misplaced?"

Professor Skoczek tapped his lips with his index finger. They had come to another long traffic light.

"This morning, Szprotka went missing. What's happened to her or where she is, I have no idea. She's vanished." He snapped his fingers. The light changed and they crossed.

"Cats like to go out, Professor. It's their 'wild' nature to hunt and carouse."

"I understand, Doctor, but Szprotka only goes out on a leash. It's safer and she's never minded. As we live on the fourth floor, there is no easy way for her to come and go without me. Until today, she has been content to stay in our apartment or to go out on a leash in my company."

"All the more reason to seize the opportunity for freedom."

"It doesn't feel like that. Szprotka has gotten out and

explored the parking lot, but she's always been hesitant about approaching the street. Of her own free will she's run back to the building after a half-hour or so. She's certainly never stayed out an entire day."

"I see, Professor. Szprotka is missing and you're worried she may be in need."

"Yes, Doctor. I'm concerned for her well-being."

"Rightly, Professor." They came to Rynek and sat on a park bench. Doctor Lighthouse unsnapped Piwo's leash. He snorted and bounded a short distance. "How may I be of assistance?"

"Might you use your abilities to deduce where she could be?"

"You don't think Szprotka will come home of her own accord?"

"If she was going to come home on her own, she would have by now."

"Very well, Professor, let's see what we can divine about your wayward girl." Doctor Lighthouse folded her hands in her lap and closed her eyes. Piwo came and sat between her legs. Sensing the seriousness of the situation, he laid down on the doctor's and the professor's feet.

A minute passed. Neither spoke. The only sound in the still night air was Doctor Lighthouse's slow and steady breathing. Professor Skoczek closed his eyes and thought about Szprotka. He saw her sitting at the window looking out, scratching at the door when she wanted to roam the hallway and lying on his desk watching him work. When he opened his eyes, Doctor Lighthouse still had hers closed, hands folded in her lap. A minute later she quivered and rolled her shoulders as if startled from a deep sleep. Piwo sat up and looked at her.

"What have you ascertained, doctor?"

"Szprotka is close." Professor Skoczek nodded. "She is safe and not injured or harmed in any way."

Professor Skoczek nodded again. "That is good news."

"She is confused though. Now that she's gotten to where she is, she can't find her way back."

"She can't come back the way she went and there is no other way out?"

"Yes, but there will be a happy ending, I am certain."

"How do you know, doctor?"

"I saw an angel hovering above Szprotka."

"An angel." A tear came to his eye. "That *is* a good sign."

"Indeed, Professor, and when I asked the angel where Szprotka was, the angel said, 'Listen to the voice from above'."

"'Listen to the voice from above'. What does that mean, Doctor?"

"On one level, dear professor, it means listen to yourself, your inner voice, and in another sense...I'm not certain." Professor Skoczek grasped the Doctor's hands.

"So, we know she's safe and she can't get home and I need to listen to a voice, my own, from above?"

"It is a riddle, professor. The words of the angel are clear, but we must understand them in a way we normally don't. The angel is asking us to explore the paradigm shift she has presented us with."

"I must put my mind to it in a way I haven't yet." Professor Skoczek looked heavenward. Doctor Lighthouse followed his lead. The pair sat in silence, searching the star-lit sky, listening with their hearts.

"Good evening, professor," the triplets, Renata, Agata and Beata said, turning their gazes to the night sky.

"Good evening, girls," Professor Skoczek replied.

"We are on our way to Club Cool," they said.

"Our boyfriends are in a band," Agata on the left said.

"They're playing tonight," Beata in the middle said.

"They're going to be rock stars," Renata on the right said.

"Fantastic. Girls, this is my good friend, Doctor

Lighthouse."

"Good evening." The girls smiled and curtsied.

"'Lovely to meet you," Doctor Lighthouse said.

"Renata, Agata, Beata," Professor Skoczek said, not making hand-indications as to which of the triplets each name was meant for. "These girls are my best students."

Doctor Lighthouse smiled and nodded.

"We don't think so," the girls said.

"Ah, but you *must think* you are good," Doctor Lighthouse said. "Otherwise, you will never *allow* yourselves to *be* good."

"That makes sense," Beata in the middle said.

"I will try to remember that," Renata, on her right, said.

"I am going to write it down so I don't forget," Agata, on her left said, producing a notebook and pen from her knapsack.

"Szprotka is home?" Renata said, looking from the professor to the doctor. Professor Skoczek shook his head.

"No, not yet."

"Oooh." the triplets groaned.

"We looked for her on our way home," Renata said.

"Then in the park after dinner and schoolwork," Agata said.

"We can look for her now, if you like," Beata offered.

"It isn't necessary," Professor Skoczek said. "Doctor Lighthouse assures me everything will work out."

"How do you know, Doctor?" the girls asked.

"An angel told me," Doctor Lighthouse said with a twinkle in her eye.

"We'll meet at your apartment in the morning before school as promised, professor."

"You girls get to Club Cool and have fun. Szprotka will be fine, I am certain.

"See you in the morning, professor," Agata said.

"At a quarter to eight at your apartment," Renata added.

"We'll be there," Beata vowed.

"Nice to meet you," they said to Doctor Lighthouse, curtsying again.

"And you," the Doctor said.

The triplets continued across Rynek Square, singing one of their boyfriends' songs, the lyrics being, "See those girls who look the same. I can't tell you each one's name."

After a pause, Professor Skoczek said, "I should be getting back. I have homework to correct. May I walk you to Café Irlandia, doctor?"

"Thank you." She stood. "Come along Piwo. We're going to the park." Piwo barked as she snapped his leash on. "I'm glad I could help. I'm sure Szprotka will come home."

"Yes. I am, too."

At the corner, they crossed without waiting for the light. A man indicated his dissatisfaction with their inappropriate behavior and Professor Skoczek and Doctor Lighthouse ignored him. Piwo looked at him and grunted, sensing his negativity and meanness.

"It's only been half a day, Professor. I wouldn't worry just yet. Cats have a way of losing themselves to humans when they don't necessarily feel lost to themselves in the slightest."

"Maybe," Professor Skoczek said. "Good night, doctor."

"Good night, Professor."

Professor Skoczek started down Ulica Gliwicka (Oo-*leets*-uh Glih-*veets*-kuh), crossing against the light, walking to Rynek Square and down Piastow Bytomskych (Pee-*ah*-stoof Bih-*tom*-skee). Stepping into his building, he climbed the stairs, thinking about what Doctor Lighthouse had said.

"Listen to the voice from above." With added emphasis, Professor Sloczek repeated the phrase. "*Listen to the voice from above.* A peculiar message except it came from an angel."

Unlocking his door, he entered his apartment, secured the locks behind him and went into the kitchen, made a cup of tea, then changed into his pajamas, robe and slippers. At his desk, he sipped the hot, steamy liquid and perused his students' homework, making notes on them He then turned to his own writings, an article for an American newspaper, poems for an anthology, a short story for his collection, a chapter for a textbook and another for a novel. As he wrote, the warm, concentrated light from his desk-lamp lulled him into semi-consciousness. Placing his pencil on the desk and slouching in his chair, he half-closed his eyes, stared into the steam rising from his cup and drifted into a dream.

Pirate cannons pounded Captain Szprotka's battered, broken-masted ship as the howling scoundrels bounded over its sides onto the deck like a pack of snarling dogs, wild hair flying around their luminous silhouettes, a dying blood-red sun behind them.

Captain Szprotka's vessel limped towards the darkening horizon. The pirates had chased them all day, swooping down like birds of prey late in the afternoon. Despite her sailors' braveries, their best efforts had proven powerless against the buccaneers' frenzied advance. Like blood-thirsty monkeys swinging through the jungle on vines of human intestines, knives clenched in their teeth and pistols stuffed in their belts, the howling war-cries of the adrenalized beasts rose and fell between the cannonade explosions heaving countless shards of metal, wood and flesh into the foray. The air choked with smoke. Sailors and savages lay dying at her feet, blood running across the decks and over the sides into the deep-purple sea. Friend or foe, those fallen overboard crashed into the gaping mouths of waiting sharks.

The ships groaned like two wild animals with horns locked in deadly combat, their big guns pounding one another at point-blank range. Timber and flesh ripped and exploded slivers and chunks everywhere. Captain Szprotka stood at the ship's wheel, in a red bandana, purple-striped shirt, and blue vest and coat, in tall black boots, refusing to surrender.

"All is lost, Captain," her first mate, a scraggly, gray cat with a black eye-patch shouted. "Our only hope is for you to lay down your sword in defeat and deliver our fates into the hands of these blood-thirsty heathens."

Captain Szprotka surveyed the debacle, pirates to the fore, pirates to the aft and flanking both sides, the ship sloshing heavily from water taken on.

"All is lost. I must ring the deck bell. We must

surrender or die."

Captain Szprotka sprang to the mizzenmast and grabbed the rope beneath the signal bell, swinging it from side to side, its clanging sounding above the din of bloody, mortal combat. The fighting stumbled to a halt, the moans of the exhausted and dying settling over the shattered decks. Smoke funnelled from below, greasily ascending to heaven like tarnished angels in the trailing wind. Captain Szprotka leaped to the banister.

"In the name of God and country, to save the lives of those in my charge, I declare a complete and full surrender. All hands in my command are ordered to cease fighting and lay down their weapons."

A sigh of hard-fought dismay passed through her crew as the scrape and clink of swords and side-arms falling against the deck resonated in the chilling wind. The souls of the unfortunate shrieked a final time as they prepared to go to that place where seamen and savages meet eternity.

Captain Szprotka unsheathed her sword and handed it to a bearded, toothless rascal. The scoundrel glared at it then held it above his head, shaking it before his ship mates, letting out a howl. His victory cry echoed, carried by his beastly brethren, down the length of both vessels.

"Nothing is worth the senseless deaths of so many. I

submit, by will and force," Captain Szprotka said as her demoralized crew was herded at gun and knife-point to the pirate vessel.

"We should have fought to the death," one sailor muttered, shuttled below deck with his comrades.

Presenting himself to Szprotka, the pirate captain bowed, removing his ostrich-plumed hat and exposing a scar running the length of his head and half of his face, snarling and baring a mouthful of gold teeth.

"Captain Knickish at your service, though it is likely to be your last exchange of words in this lifetime." Captain Szprotka did not speak. "Your vessel and its bounty are mine. Your men are my prisoners. The only thing to decide is what to do with you." He glanced over the railing at the frenzy of waiting sharks.

"I only ask that my men be treated with dignity while in your capture."

Captain Knickish threw his head back and cackled. "Dignity? I'll work them 'til they're bone-dead then feed them to these lions of the sea," pointing at the rows of chainsaw teeth frothing the water below.

"As for you..." Captain Knickish motioned for his men to secure a board over the side of the boat. At his command, they formed a gauntlet, laughing and taunting and sneering with glee when Captain Knickish pointed to the board. "This is your dignity." He belly-laughed, jabbing the point of the sword into Captain Szprotka's back. Her crippled ship shuddered as wave after wave crashed against its wounded hull, making it difficult for her to keep her balance. From the blood-drenched ocean below, the sharks demanded her sacrifice, churning and splashing the sea with unsated bloodlust.

Forced to walk the length of wood arching beneath her feet, Captain Szprotka had come to the end of the plank, the point of no return. Facing the final rays of the setting sun, she breathed in what little warmth and hope they could impart. One nudge from Knickish's sword and she was off the edge, falling. The pirates cheered.

"No-o-o-o-o-o-o!" Professor Skoczek woke, the image of Szprotka tumbling with him from sleep to the reality of a new day, clawing at the air as if snatching Szprotka into his arms. Shaking with terror, he sat up and looked at his lap. Szprotka was not there.

Springing from his chair, his slippered feet carried him into the bathroom. Twisting the sink spigot, he filled his cupped hands with cold water and splashed his face once, then again, then once more. Leaning on the sink basin, he interrogated the tousled, bleary-eyed figure in the mirror.

Where is Szprotka? Is the dream an omen? Has she

really been kidnapped? Has harm come to her? Is she dead? Think Skoczek, think.

Professor Skoczek remembered what Doctor Lighthouse had said about concentrating in some way he hadn't. His best ideas often came in the bathtub, the hot water allowing his mind to bend in ways it couldn't at his desk. Turning the claw-foot's hot-water nozzle, the pipes rattled and pounded like a rocket preparing for blast-off. Steaming water rushed into the tub as fast as frightening thoughts poured into his brain.

"It's seven o'clock, time enough for a bath and some thinking." Padding into the kitchen, he made coffee and carried the cup into the bathroom's steamy wetness.

"Where could Szprotka have gotten?" Setting the cup on the table next to the tub, he lowered himself into the water, recounting the events before and after Szprotka's disappearance, closing his eyes and letting the warmth take his body and mind. *Yesterday I opened the apartment door while speaking on the phone.* Dozing hypnotically, he heard Szprotka's cry, distant, hollow, muffled. *Is this a dream?*

Twiiiiiiiing, twiiiiiiiing. The doorbell tore him from his slumber. Professor Skoczek sat up. "One minute." He climbed out of the tub and wrapped himself in a towel, hurrying to dress.

The doorbell rang again, twiiiiiiing, twiiiiiiing, and yes, it *was* Szprotka mewing above, like the angel had said, and in that moment Professor Skoczek knew where Szprotka was. Fumbling with the latches, he unlocked the door and flung it open. The triplets, Doctor Lighthouse and Piwo were standing in the hallway.

"We know where Szprotka is," the girls exclaimed, pointing up the stairs.

"I figured out what the angel meant when she said, 'listen to the voice from above'," Doctor Lighthouse added, pointing upstairs also.

"Yes, we are all correct," Professor Skoczek said, grabbing a key from a rung and leading everyone to the attic door and unlocking it. There was Szprotka, looking up and mewing happily.

Professor Skoczek lifted her to his chest. Szprotka was home.

Doctor Lighthouse said, "I realized these buildings have attics and you mentioned that workers had been in yours. Piwo and I were a block away and I thought to come tell you. A woman cleaning rugs in the parking lot let us in."

"We arrived as Doctor Lighthouse was coming into the building," Agata said.

Szprotka licked Professor Skoczek's hand and,

purring, climbed on his shoulder.

"Let's have a breakfast to celebrate the solving of 'The Theft of Szprotka'," Professor Skoczek said.

"We must get to school," Renata said, or was it Beata?

"We are having a history test about the movie our class saw yesterday," Agata said, or was it Beata or Renata?

"We hate history," Renata said, or was it one of her sisters? Professor Skoczek was positively uncertain.

"And I must get home," Doctor Lighthouse said. "I am having my apartment remodeled today, but thank you." To Szprotka she said, "Szprotka, perhaps now you won't be so eager to run away and get locked in the attic again."

Szprotka winked. The triplets patted Szprotka behind her ears, on top of her head and under her chin. With Szprotka in his arms, Professor Skoczek stood at the top of the stairs and watched his friend and students leave.

"Have a good day, professor," the triplets said.

"Yes, have a splendid day, my dear professor," Doctor Lighthouse said. Piwo snorted.

"Take care, all of you, and have a wonderful day. Thank you for your help."

His hair still wet, holding Szprotka in his arms he walked into the living room and looked at Szprotka's favorite window nook. Through the glass, he could see radiant sunlight streaming between reverberating, white clouds. He rubbed Szprotka's stomach and she rested her head on his forearm, closing her eyes and twitching her nose.

"With a little luck, Szprotka, it will be another fine day." Kissing her on the forehead, he whispered in her ear, "Kee-cha, kee-cha, little fish, you've come home."

Szprotka slipped from Professor Skoczek's arms, ran to the kitchen and, ignoring the saucers of milk and fish the professor had placed on the floor, leaped onto the table and lapped milk from the glass her master had left on the table the day before.

Blood Money

Chapter 13

Rebel's Revenge

"Um cold," Douglas, the youngest brother said, rubbing his hands together and wiping his nose with his coat-sleeve. At thirteen, the War had been a game, laying in the grass or hiding in a tree, shooting then running like children playing hide-and-seek.

Having not eaten since yesterday morning, the brothers had a gnawing in their bellies, a fusion of hunger and fear.

Today Douglas wanted the game to be over. He dreamed of a solid meal, a soft bed and his father to be with them again.

"'What chuh git fer runnin' off tih be uh hero," Buck, his eldest brother, said. At seventeen, Buck was the wisest of the three, his mood the darkest. His brothers looked to him for acknowledgment of what they did, how they did it, the reasons for doing it and how to feel afterwards. The battle, perhaps even the war, would be over today. They looked to Buck for one last cup of courage.

Buck's hands and shoulders were those of a man. Their father dead, he'd strapped on the plough and laid his back against the harness, furrowing the hard, rocky ground despite the crops comprehending the futility of poking their heads into human conflict.

Nothing good'd come from the War though everyone had been crazy to get it started. No one had foreseen that Confederates firing on the federal garrison at Fort Sumter would bring the nation to its knees. Spectators brought picnic baskets and sat on hilltops to watch the battles when the War first broke. Now it was insanity to look, or to turn away. The depths of madness both sides had been driven to were dark and deadly. The Devil was dancing a jig and nothing in their time on earth had prepared the three boys for this, hunkered on a ridge, the enemy amassing at the bottom of the hill. No yesterday, no tomorrow, everything would be decided today.

Buck brushed the scar on his cheek where a home guardsman, one of the townsmen who'd stayed in the village to make certain everyone tramped off to war, had smashed him with the butt-end of a mud-caked 1853 British Enfield rifle. That was before his father'd been killed. 'Til then, he'd been undecided.

"Whatever's gonna' happen is what's gonna' be." After their father's death, Buck was finished with words. What he wanted was revenge.

Douglas tried to read his oldest brother's body language. It was as if a poisonous snake had worked its way into Buck and was hiding inside. Waiting. He hadn't allowed himself to cry. He was the man now. Men did what had to be done.

Like the thousands of others trapped in the hellish conflagration, the brothers were lean and sullen, skin caked with battle-smoke and dirt as if the soil they'd cared for was demanding their blood as punishment for what Buck had forced them to become. Too young to understand mortality, Douglas hummed *Johnny Reb*, the fight song that had bolstered their mercurial confidence.

On their stomachs, they peered down from the bluff listening to the Northern soldiers crossing the river in the pre-dawn darkness. Their enemy, Cranston's Blue Brigadiers, was renowned for their fighting skills and 'never surrender' attitude. It was the splashes made clambering out of their boats that betrayed their stealthy approach, setting fear in every Rebel on the ridge. What could be heard was far more ominous than what could not be seen.

"This here's it, ain't it, Buck?" Frederick, the middle brother said. Buck leaned against Douglas, tugging Douglas' cap down over his brother's dull eyes, then looked at Frederick on his other side.

"Damn straight, little brother. Gonna' give 'ese Yankees hell this mornin'."

"I'm a'feared," Douglas said, sniffling in the bone-chilling, pre-dawn cold, wishing he could will everything back to the summer of 1859.

"Ain't nothin' tih be a'feared' of, little brother," Buck said. "Yih jist got tuh git yore rear-end home and tell Ma to kill a chicken and fix us lunch. Frederick 'n' me'll join yih afore the sun's high in the sky."

Frederick wondered where any of them would be at morning's end. Buck winked at Douglas. "'Ar feet'll be beatin' the porch rails afore you ken' ring thuh lunch bell." He looked up at the sky. "We're gonna' sit down tih biscuits an' gravy an' everythin'. Ain't that right, Frederick?" Buck formed his fingers into a pistol and aimed them at Frederick. Frederick lowered his head, breathing like a man choking on his own blood.

The Confederates had been driven onto this ridge-top yesterday when the Union soldiers'd swept in. Savaged by yesterday's invasion, what was left of Shokenaw, their hometown, commanded its sons to exact retribution.

According to Confederate spies, half of Cranston's men had crossed, the other half still on the far bank. The union army divided, it was attack now and kill enough Yankees to drive the Blue Coats away for good or wait for combined federal forces to march up this hill and slaughter every last Confederate. For Buck, the latter was unacceptable. Their father's memory would die.

Hell-bent on a quick run up the grassy slope, Union officers planned a complete and merciless slaughter of every confederate-at-arms. Desperate for victory, anything else would be defeat.

"Closest yeh can git tih God in this whole county," the boys' father had said of this forested ridge. They'd hunted quail together here on those warm summer days that promised everything good would last forever. This morning's unfoldings were overwhelming cause for doubt.

Their father, Amos Withers, had gone to fight the Blues the summer before and was anonymously killed during three bloody days of intense Gettysburg fighting. A makeshift gravestone next to their house read *Amos Withers: January 4th, 1827—July 1st-3rd, 1863—Husband of Dottie, father of Buck, Frederick and Douglas—Good father, husband, farmer and soldier.* Buck had carved it. It had taken an entire afternoon. He hadn't wanted to finish, knowing that when he laid his whittling knife down he'd take up arms and in defense of his rage, his father's death would be avenged. "An eye for an eye," the good Book said.

Running for their lives yesterday and reassembling on this ridge today, the three boys clung to the notion it *was* the closest place to God. Buck believed it was where his rage would finally find a home.

His father's death had pounded in his ears; against his mother's wishes, he'd snuck away, taking his brothers with him. Rage had blackened his heart, such that what he lacked in wisdom he bluffed with bravado…until today. The line between heaven and earth had been drawn.

Buck had four notches on his sniper's rifle. Frederick had two, having earned his second by killing a boy between his and Buck's age. The musket ball'd thunked into the boy's chest and sent him flying backwards in a spray of purple blood, tearing flesh and tender bone. Mortally wounded, he begged for water, crying for his mother and his home. Buck spat in the gaping chest hole, the boy choking on Yankee blood and Confederate spit. Frederick had fallen to his knees, dry-heaving as Buck carved the second notch in his brother's rifle-butt.

Douglas had closed his eyes each time he'd fired. He'd chucked up tree bark and dirt, but it felt appeasing and he couldn't say why.

"Y'all comin'?" Douglas said, hesitating, awaiting his brother's fateful reply.

"Frederick an' me got business with eez Yankees. We'll be home faster'n a cricket runs from a broomstick switch. You git goin' now. Run the ridge 'til yeh come to Barker's Trail. Foller it down till yeh git outta' these woods then take that jacket and hat off and mosey on like you wuz the Lord's shepherd bringin' His sheep home."

"What about 'ar snipers?" Douglas asked.

"Yih know all th' calls, 'n' most uh their names," Buck said. "Run fer five seconds, stop an' give th' signal. Yeh'll be alright, now go." Buck shoved Douglas to get him started. Douglas snatched up his rifle.

"C'mon, Rabbit," Douglas said to the hound resting at their feet. Rabbit shot a glance at Buck. She was his dog. She looked at him with perked ears as if to say, "I'll do whatever you tell me."

"Rabbit's gonna' bite a Yankee on the ass and taste Bluecoat flesh. We'll bring a chunk home in a handkerchief. You kin scare yer girlfriends with it."

Frederick laughed like a tree branch scratching a

window pane. Douglas tried to smile, but his jaw was set like the scarecrow their mother had made to keep the crows away. A Yankee had trampled it yesterday. Everyone was angry these days, going at each other like rabid dogs.

"Why's zis' 'bout slaves?" Frederick asked. "Pa never owned nobody fer nuthin."

"'Tain't about slaves," Buck said. "'It's 'bout damned side-burned tailcoats makin' Southern folks give up ever'theen' and get nuthin' fer it. Damned Yankee's never got 'nuff uv anything." He leveled his rifle and pointed it at the river. "An' it's fer Pa." He pretended to fire, mimicking the kick in his shoulder.

People said angels hovered over the ridge that day, their sweet singing interrupted by the harsh sound of the long guns firing from beyond the river. Douglas saw angels hovering above his brothers' heads. Years later, he'd tell it that way.

"Drop yer weapon and git goin'," Buck commanded. "'Can't run with no rifle." Douglas laid it on the ground between his brothers.

"Tell Ma we love 'er and we'll be home soon," Frederick said.

The angel-song was louder. So were the metallic whines of artillery shells arcing overhead.

"Go," Buck ordered. Douglas bolted into the high grass behind them and was gone.

Frederick and Buck stared at the spot where Douglas had disappeared. A moment later, a cannon ball ripped a gaping hole in the ridge in front of them.

"He'll be okay?" Frederick asked.

"Better than runnin' inta' th' devil-world we're 'bout teh."

"We ain't reg'lar soldiers, Buck. We done a little snipin,' but we ain't never killed a man up close. Snipin' ain't real soldier'n, hidin' 'hind a rock, shootin' 'n' runnin'. Les' drop ur guns and go home wi' Douglas."

"Won't be no home to git to if we don't swoop down here, bite some Yankee ears off 'n' spit 'em in their faces. Ain't gonna' be no end 'til I get a mouthful of Yankee blood." With those words, he sealed his brother's fate.

"Ah don't know," Frederick said, running his hand up and down his rifle.

"Don't need teh know, little brother. Just got teh do," Buck said, cocking the percussion hammer. Buck looked at his brother. "It's in God's hands now," he said, looking up and nodding.

Frederick inched closer to his older brother. Rabbit sidled between them. A shell thudded and exploded in front of them, throwing dirt in their faces and numbing their ears. Rabbit whimpered.

"Looks like stars on the water, don' it, Buck?" Frederick said, pointing at the river reflecting the shell-bursts like Fourth of July fireworks. The eastern horizon was a red patina, foreshadowing the day, men on both sides certain God was on *theirs*.

"In between stars an' Heaven, little brother." Buck put a hand on Rabbit's head and rubbed it like a magic lamp then did the same to Frederick.

Fate came in two words. "Ready weapons," the sergeant yelled. Both boys exhaled at the same time. Buck shifted his hand to the back of Frederick's neck. Frederick looked into Rabbit's eyes, then his brother's. The Confederate troops behind them were pressing forward.

"See yeh at th' bottom, soldier," Buck said. His smile twisted into a grimace. Frederick's mouth crumbled to a jagged grin.

The time for talking gone, there was nothing left to say, not even what would make everyone see how wrong all this was. Like so many other boys that day, in one moment Frederick and Buck passed from childhood to man, musket balls sizzling overhead. Shells screeched. The ground shook. Their world erupted into a blinding, searing hell.

A ghastly thud sounded behind them. Like a log dropping, their sergeant collapsed backwards, shredded to pieces by a shell that had made its mark.

As they pushed their way over the embankment, their souls abandoned their mortal coils to join their father here on Sugarbeet Ridge.

Frederick tripped or fell. A flood of rebels swept down the bluff bellowing like banshees, carrying Buck in its tide. Bullets whizzed and thudded, clotting puffs of dust and smoke. Rabbit ran step for step with Buck until a musket ball ripped into her master's chest, catching Buck's astonishment before he went limp, crumpling like a piece of laundry in a backyard breeze. Buck saw his father's reflection in Rabbit's eyes before his own glazed.

Gravity and the gods took his soul, his body slamming into a tree, a haggard lump among countless others. A rebel coming down gave Rabbit a tail-up kick and she ran baying Man's inhumanity to Man all the way to the river. There'd be chicken and gravy waiting for her if she could find her way home, and she'd be Douglas' dog now, if he'd made it safe too.

Blood Money

Chapter 14

Circle 'Round New Mexico

Take the Desert Train
Down to Santa Fe
Meet me in the square
We'll go dancing there
And fall in love

- The Twisters

"Hold on to your teeth and kiss your hat good-bye," Nez said, shooting road-buddy Rocky's gray Honda Accord south out of Denver down US 25, instigating their Santa-Fe-New-Mexico-Fourth-of-July long-weekend magical-mystery-tour. In his early thirties, at five-feet-ten-and-a-half inches, Nez was graced with one hundred sixty pounds of lean, athletic muscle. Sporting orange running shoes, plaid tourist shorts, a sleeveless white t-shirt and blood-red forehead bandana that hugged his dark-brown pigtails, he projected raw, vigorous youthfulness.

His stone-carved cheekbones and nose imparting a leading-man look, Rocky exuded the ruggedness of the mountains he was named for, walking and talking like he knew what he was doing even when unsure where his next step would land. Happiest wandering Southwestern back-roads with Nez, they were a Don Quixote/Sancho Panzo dynamic duo. Rocky wore dark colors all year-round, summer's heat not affecting him like it did Nez.

Their Austin-based, transcendental-healer friend, Virgina Parker, had landed a past-life-reformation teaching position at Ojo Caliente (*Oh*-ho Cal-ee-*en*-tay) Mineral Hot Springs in New Mexico and had invited Nez and Rocky down for some spiritual invigoration, offering to chaperone their holiday adventure. Neither Rocky nor Nez knew what awaited, but were glad to be on the road, looking forward to whatever the spirits and Virginia's guidance held for them.

They'd met her a month prior at the Kerrville Folk Festival southwest of Austin, Texas, out in Jimmie Rodgers hill country. In the wee hours, Nez and Rocky were strolling from tent-camp to tent-camp, guitars slung over their shoulders like journeymen with the tools of their trade strapped to their backs, joining whoever invited them to pick and sing. At the bottom of Hanging

Tree Hill, Nez was banging out some hill-country blues with two hardcore Texas Toasters, the nickname he'd given the 'locals,' when Rocky drifted into the shadows of thinning moonlight and returned with the lovely and ultra-dimensional Virginia Parker at his side.

A tall, slender, honey-blonde beauty, Virginia's Winnie-the-Pooh eyes exuded dark mystery and sweet innocence. Nez spotted her earlier in the evening at the guitar-giveaway booth at the back of the main-stage audience. Wearing a red and yellow festival t-shirt and dangerously short denim cut-offs, she was sat in a high-backed rocking chair rolled back in extreme, pushing rhythmically with her cowgirl boots against the booth railing in time to the music.

The give-away guitar was a brand new, blonde Martin. She was blonde and brand new too. Their eyes met and Nez's soul did a 'wuh,' his heart beating faster. Picking up the guitar and strumming it, he imagined holding Virginia and strumming her. The wood reverberated against his chest. He, Virginia and the give-away guitar were in tune with the Universe.

At three in the morning under a Hanging Tree Hill moon, Rocky and Virginia entered the campfire-light sharing a laugh—a tempered squeal on her part, a full-blown Midwestern charmer on his. Virginia's voice arched and peaked like the last strain of a pre-dawn coyote howl, culminating in an even richer, fuller, more soulful squeal. *That woman sure can squeal*, Nez thought, liking her twice as much as when he'd met her at the booth.

The trio stumbled through the last strains of June-moon Texas folk music and crawled into their sleeping bags at five a.m. to rest for several hours.

Next morning, Virginia wrangled official Kerrville Folk Festival staff food for her friends and took them to a local swimming hole on the Medina River, where, standing in the waist-deep water, she squealed as the tiny, silver fish nipped at her legs. Nez wished he was one, liking her twice as much as the twice as much from the previous evening.

She talked about Atlantis and Lemuria, lost continents said to exist eons ago, speaking of them as if from first-hand experience. Nez got the sense she *was from* at least one of the fabled continents and could travel there whenever she desired, slipping through an extraterrestrial dimension at the wink of an eye or nip of a fish. She was an ancient, fun-loving soul and Nez was in line to buy a ticket for the journey.

Virginia had a way of holding her hand on her hip that made Nez want to look at her until both died and went to each other's heaven or Las Vegas for an Elvis-chapel wedding then on to a Nepalese honeymoon on a Kathmandu cloud. She was a Texas humdinger.

The plan was to meet in Old Town Square, Santa Fe, at four p.m. today, the Fourth of July.

At Happy Canyon, Colorado, Nez opened the car up. The town of Castle Rock came and went. Nez knew the locations of the speed traps ahead and slowed to fifty-five at Colorado Springs. Four different police cars, each hosting a uniformed officer with a hand-held radar device, whisked past Rocky's Honda. Thinking they'd out-smarted the Smokies, Nez sped up after the fourth, accelerating to seventy-five in a fifty-five zone. A fifth patrol car appeared and pulled to the side as they rolled over the final rise south out of town. Glancing in the side mirror, he was surprised when it didn't come charging after them. They were damn lucky or blessed, which was, to Nez's current thinking, the same thing.

Rocky took the wheel south of Pueblo, where Interstate 25 turns into the original Santa Fe Trail, driving through Walsenburg to Trinidad, Colorado, gateway to New Mexico and home of Emily's Truck Stop.

Emily was wearing a red-flowered Hawaiian shirt beneath her full-length, white apron and smiling despite not having her false teeth in. Nez imagined them in a cup on a nightstand or stashed in a drawer.

"How was Hawaii?" a trucker sitting on a red-topped chrome stool at the counter said. She'd recently returned and was eager to tell everyone about the trip.

"It was wonderful. We wore grass skirts and coconut brassieres and danced the hula on Waikiki beach (*Why*-kee-kee = a popular beach on the Hawaiian island of Oahu). We took pictures." She handed them to the trucker. Turning to Nez and Rocky she said, "What'll you boys have this morning?"

"Chicken-fried steak," Rocky said without hesitation. Nez ordered the breakfast special: two eggs sunny-side up, one strip of bacon, two sausage links, three pancakes, coffee, grapefruit juice, hash browns and two pieces of buttered wheat toast. Emily forgot the toast, but Nez didn't mention it.

When he'd eaten everything on his plate, Nez went into the gift shop and saw a baseball cap that said, "My wife ran off with my best friend and I really miss him." He put it on his head and examined his reflection in the mirror from several angles, then set it back on the rack. Rocky found some cocktail coasters with amorous sayings on them, the best being, "Be careful or I'll include you in all my plans."

"Pay for those trinkets and let's get on the road,"

Nez said.

Rising over Raton Pass like a winged phoenix, they eased to a gentle landing in New Mexico, Land of Enchantment, passing through Springer, Tecolote and Bernal, rationing one eye-blink for each. Soon after noon, south of Glorieta they saw a cumulus cloud shaped like a bear paw holding a heart in its claws and took it as a sign of good fortune, an omen of the spiritual and secular adventures awaiting them.

"We're blessed in the wine of the Lord," Nez said.

"She knows we can use it."

"A blessing or some wine?"

"Both," Rocky said, adding his laughter to Nez's.

Nez recalled a story a friend once told him and recounted it to Rocky.

"I had a friend named Louie who hitchhiked through here. One morning he woke with a rattlesnake in his sleeping bag. Louie said he laid there all day until nightfall when the air cooled and the snake slithered out."

"Good thing it was only once," Rocky said.

"Hearing that story or sharing your sleeping bag with a snake?"

"Both," Rocky said. They laughed again.

A green highway sign said *Santa Fe—Saint Frances Drive - 2nd Exit—Old Town Square*. It was already 4:30

p.m.; Virginia would have likely been waiting for them for half an hour. Rocky directed the Honda onto the exit ramp and eased it into the parking lot behind the Pink Adobe Restaurant. Walking several blocks to the red-white-and-blue decorated Old Town Square, it was packed with Hispanics, Native Americans and Caucasians of all kinds. Nez made a beeline to the bandstand on the far side of the square. Rocky followed.

"I'll find her," Nez said.

"I'll be over there on the curb sketching with my chalks." Rocky pointed to where the parade would come around the corner. He was good with chalks.

Nez climbed the bandstand stairs, walked center-stage and tapped the podium microphone. Tipping his sunglasses to make eye contact with a crisply-uniformed, highly-decorated National Guard General staring at him from the side of the stage, Nez held one hand up in a Hollywood Indian greeting, extending the other in a white-man-style handshake. The general flailed *his* arms as if signaling he might like to surrender.

"With your permission, General, I'd like to page a friend."

Looking left and right and finding no one with whom to take up the matter, the general shrugged.

"We're down from Denver to rendezvous with our

handler at sixteen hundred hours." Nez checked his watch. Liking the sound of 'sixteen hundred hours' military time, the general issued a 'yes' head-shake.

People at the front of the bandstand watched Nez, the Indian and the General, wondering if the show had begun. A few thought one was going to get scalped, but were unsure which. Since the race riots of the 60s, American blacks and whites feigned "racial equality." In New Mexico, Native Americans, Hispanics and Caucasians were walking their own fine line of ethnic inter-relation.

A photo journalist snapped a picture of Nez and the General standing shoulder to shoulder shaking hands, then Nez spoke into the microphone: "Paging Virginia Parker, Princess of Lemuria. Please come to the main stage. Your party has arrived," adding, "And I *do mean party,*" to applause.

A sun-baked woman in tight jeans, Stetson cowboy hat and denim shirt decorated with silver and turquoise jewelry tugged at Nez's foot. "And Hilda Mayo, too."

Nez gripped the microphone like Elvis Presley. "Hilda Mayo, come on down. We can't start the show without you." The woman nodded her thanks and smiled as if she was thirty years younger. The crowd parted and Virginia, hand on hip, walked towards Nez as he saluted the General.

"Love what you've done with the Square." Not waiting for the General's reply, he leaped from the stage to more applause, meeting Virginia halfway.

"How are you, Princess?" Nez gave her a hug that made his head and heart flutter like a school boy's first kiss.

"Best as ever," she said, returning the hug.

"You look prettier than new paint on an old tractor."

Virginia squealed.

"That's a great squeal ya' got there, Princess. Rocky's over there drawing with his chalks." Nez pointed across the square.

The parade was rounding the corner when Nez and Virginia got to him. Rocky was sitting on the curb, sketching the jewelry artisans hawking their wares across the street in front of the Governor's Palace, a bronze plaque claiming it as the oldest building in the United States. Posing arm-in-arm in the middle of the parade route in Rocky's line of vision, Rocky sketched them in until a policeman shooed them onto the sidewalk. Packing his chalks and drawing pad in his satchel, he hugged Virginia.

Virginia squealed.

"That's a great squeal ya' got there, Princess."

"That's what your partner tells me. I want to introduce you to a friend of mine at the Ore House. She works at the Light Institute down by Cerrillos (Sir-*ree*-ose). You'll like her."

Slipping an arm around each, she led them across the square, up the Ore House stairs, into the Southwest-rugged, main room and out onto the wooden-railed veranda overlooking Old Town Square.

"Raven, these are my friends from Denver, Rocky and Nez."

Raven stood. It had been some time since Nez had seen a woman wearing a turquoise-sequined dress, let alone a woman wearing a sequin dress of *any* color. Five-ten with short-cropped hair spiked like a crown, her green eyes were a mythical ocean, the pupils never focusing, like waves tiding and ebbing to the moon's pull. Fists on her hips, she looked like a super-hero ready to save the world. Nez wondered if she could breathe fire. Perhaps she'd teach him to walk on it or lay down in it with him and transform into one rarified, pure-energy being. Their waitress, Jersey, a tall, East-Coast-Jewish transplant, brought a pitcher of beer. She and Nez shared smiles. Nez admired her lanky stride as she departed.

"What's the Light Institute?" Nez asked Raven, reeling himself back to earth as he swigged the icy-cold nectar.

"A center for metaphysical studies. We send light to the Universe every Wednesday and Sunday. I've learned so much about auras and the meanings of their colors these last two years." Raven talked about Nostradamus. "He was a fifteenth-century prophet who looked into a bowl of water and divined the future in quatrainic anagrams. He predicted events up through the next century. For instance, the Antichrist was born in the Middle East on February 24th, 1966. He's studied computers, philosophy and literature, is charming and eloquent and by 1999 will be prominent in Middle Eastern politics."

"I read an article about a woman who channeled Nostradamus," Virginia said. "He told her we've been interpreting him all wrong."

"I heard about her," Raven said. "We're on this vortex time-line. The Antichrist is inevitable, but if we project light to the universe, live a sweet life and have sweet dreams, his influence will be diminished." Nez wanted to ask if Nostradamus had quatrained anything about the Buffalo coming back, but Raven announced it was time to head out to a Fourth-of-July-Firecracker-Blessing-of-the-Land Party on the high-desert hilltop property of a friend. Promising not to beam to another level without taking Rocky, Nez, and Virginia with her, they agreed to meet in the Pink Adobe parking lot.

Three cars headed south out of Santa Fe on Interstate 25 to State 14, through Cerrillos and Madrid. Five miles further, they turned right, onto a rutted, dirt road.

"Gotta' go into the badlands to get the good news," Rocky said.

"Don't let Coyote trick me again," Nez told him.

Several more miles and the caravan rolled to a stop on Los Cobreros (Coh-*brair*-rose = Coppersmith) Mesa, a top-hat-style butte overlooking Albuquerque to the Southeast and Los Alamos to the Southwest.

Getting out first, Raven declared, *"This is the place,"* waving her arms at a hole in the ground in the center of the plateau. Her friend, Norm, had denuded the area of trees, back-hoed a basement and laid the foundation for a round house for himself and his son. Having a PhD in forestry, Raven had helped. Norm had a thousand dollars worth of fireworks to bless the house and land.

"Let's do a set," Nez said. He and Rocky pulled their guitars from the trunk of the Honda and played and sang as the fireworks exploded overhead, the fading tracers raining down. Afterwards, everyone gathered around a flatbed truck for a Southwestern smorgasbord of tacos, burritos and chimichangas doused with salsa, sour cream and guacamole, washed down with liberal amounts of sangria.

It was ten-thirty when they headed back to the main road for Santa Fe. They'd said goodnight to Raven in the parking lot of the tavern in Madrid. *The white witch of the West*, Nez thought as her tail-lights faded into the darkness.

He'd made a date to rendezvous with Jersey, the waitress from the Ore House. The plan was to meet at eleven at Rodeo Nights, Santa Fe's disco honky-tonk. From the Honda's magic trunk came Nez and Rocky's cowboy hats. Walking ahead, Nez blasted into the discotheque's hoot and clamor, scanning the gyrating bodies to ascertain she wasn't there. It wasn't even country music. It was Animal Night and everyone was dancing to funk.

The trio headed to Virginia's room at the Silent Indian Hotel, a two-story, white-washed, adobe hacienda. The room was off-white with a single bed, a compact chest of drawers, a kitchenette table and one straight-backed wooden chair like the one Virginia had been sitting on at the Kerrville festival. Nez would have felt at home except for the shower-only bathroom. A bath-man more often than not, he resigned himself to being rained on before sleeping.

Virginia took the bed, Rocky fell asleep in the middle of the room on the floor and Nez wrapped himself in his royal-blue-with–white-stars blanket and nestled in the corner by the window. As he passed from waking to dreaming he thought about the newborn kittens his cat had given birth to two days ago. He'd left food and water, and the window open, so momma-cat, Lena, could come and go as she pleased. Asleep, he dreamed of Janice, the woman he had once loved.

In his dream, he was standing at the edge of a hill. The land sloped in every direction to flat, New Mexican desert and he wondered how he could be dreaming of a place he was seeing for the first time, such was the effect his New Mexican adventure was having.

A hard-packed road ran down the hill. Wearing a short, black, sleeveless nightgown, Janice floated up in long, even steps. One step from him, she stopped. He leaned forward and placed his hands on her shoulders.

For the first time in his dreams he had the sensation of touch. He could *feel* her flesh in his hands. The closure to their love was in her eyes. In his arms, but a world away in someone else's, this was their letting go. Holding her this last time stole his breath. He awoke, the feel of her skin on his fingertips. Brushing tears from his cheeks, he showered, letting it wash his sadness away. Giving her to the heavens, he joined Rocky and Virginia at the table. Accepting the past, on good terms with the present and eager for today's adventure, Nez said, "Good morning. It's great to be alive."

"Life's good and gettin' better," Rocky said.

Virginia squealed.

Breakfast was water and fruit, watermelon, grapes, apples, oranges and nectarines. They ate and planned the day.

Leaving Virginia's car at the Silent Indian Hotel, they drove north on I-25 to the healing waters of Montezuma Hot Springs west of Las Vegas, New Mexico.

There were two steaming pools, the first, hot-but-bearable, the other, wicked igneous. An aged Native American man up to his neck in the second smiled as Virginia, Rocky and Nez descended the sloping, graveled path. Nez put a cassette tape in Virginia's boom-box and Gregorian "om" sounds flirted with the spring's rhythmic gurgles. Rocky had plum wine in a leather bota bag.

"We're headed in the right direction," Rocky said like a guru about to achieve enlightenment and a gold-miner about to strike gold. He handed the boda bag to

Nez and Nez baptized his liver with a long draught.

The orange sun against the purple-red mountains and crystalline blue sky made Nez think of a Georgia O'Keefe landscape. Seeing New Mexico in person, he understood her inspiration.

As they prepared to enter the healing waters, Harley Davidson engine sounds echoed from the parking lot above, heralding the arrival of a New Mexican biker gang, grain-alcohol-fueled Valkyries in leather and motorcycle boots. Silencing their heavy-metal horses, three bikers descended the path, smashing the day's serenity with a raucous oration of vindictive obscenities.

"This water's too fucking hot, man," the first biker yelped, dipping a tattooed arm in the hot-but-bearable pool.

"Get fucking *in*, man," the second biker ordered, like a combat squad sergeant to a fighter who'd shown a sliver of fear.

"No fucking way, man. It's too fucking hot." The tattooed men jostled like kids daring each other to leap from a cliff into a swimming hole.

"Watch fucking out, man. You're going to knock me fucking in," a third biker said, peeling off his leather jacket and t-shirt to reveal a torso of surreal skin-illustrations from neck to wrists and waist. Larger and more physically-defined than the other two, he flexed one pectoral muscle then the other, asserting muscle Morse-code authority and signaling that, for their own perpetuation more than mere safety, they'd be wise to humbly step back from the pool. "No more fucking games here, d'you hear?" Turning to the pathway leading down from the parking lot, he said. "You bitches coming or not?"

Silent and emotionless, their biker women traversed the graveled incline and emerged from the brush at the bottom of the trail like off-duty sirens taking a break from luring sailors to their rocky demise, positioning themselves next to their respective men. Blowing languid menthol-cigarette smoke rings and rolling their eyes, they folded and unfolded their arms only to puff. Morse-code Man's woman had "Property of Preacher" tattooed on her neck, a not-so-subtle indication of whom she spent her time with and the nature of their relationship.

Foregoing the advantages of the hot-but-bearable pool, Nez lowered himself in beside the Indian. Wary of the bikers' intentions, Rocky escorted Virginia to the far side of the igneous pool.

Immersed in volcanic bliss, Nez remembered how his high school Civics Studies teacher, Mr. Polonoli, had taught himself to make hot water feel cool. "I make myself *believe* the water is cool and think about the color blue." Through the steam, Nez looked up at the sky.

"That's fucking okay, man," the second biker said, deflecting his peers' focus from his trepidations about getting in. The first biker stripped to his Fruit-of-the-Looms.

"My uncle used to do this. He said, 'Tell yourself the water's cool and think of the color blue'." Slithering into the water, he settled between Nez and the Indian.

Aquatically-suspended like ensemble swimmers in an Ethel Merman movie, the trio floated facing one another, arms splayed on the pool's curved lip, staring into the water between them with a common vision inspired by the hot spring's healing effects. Virginia sat on the top rung of the ladder and dangled her legs in half way up her calves. The steam commingled with her perfume. The men inhaled in unison, lighter in heart and finer in spirit.

"It cleanses the soul," she said, looking at Rocky and Nez then the Indian and the biker, surmising who was ready for a trip to Atlantis. The Indian grinned like the New Mexican sun.

"It's fucking okay, man," the biker said, and no one said anything until the biker spoke again. "That's fucking enough for me, man." He climbed out and Rocky moved to the edge of the pool, reclining on his side.

"It's preparation for fire-walking," Nez said, breathing like an alligator with its nose, eyes and head barely above the water's surface. Rocky stuck his hand in.

"It's hot."

"Thousands of people, millions have done this," Nez said. Taking a double-swig of purple wine, Rocky moved to the ladder and positioned himself at the top as Virginia lowered herself in. "Get the good news," Nez said. Rocky submerged himself to his chin. Everyone sighed, surrendering their troubles to the sun and the surrounding mountains, the water's heat permeating their bodies and spirits.

Time passed. No one could say how long. Nez bellied up to the edge and laid his forearms on the pool's concrete ledge. Virginia floated to Rocky. Hovering six inches from his face, she giggled, sank to the bottom of the pool like a mermaid returning to Lemuria, then broke surface like a breaching whale, running her hands through her hair and spewing a mouthful of water.

"You are a hot springs princess," Rocky said, Nez and the Indian nodding agreement.

Virginia squealed.

The Indian moved to the ladder and pulled himself out. Facing the sun, he whispered and touched his forehead, lips and heart, raising his arms to the golden New Mexican day, uttering a prayer in what might have been Lumerian. He looked at Nez and started down the valley. Nez pulled himself up on the edge of the pool to watch. The Indian stepped into the creek and did a handstand, head and chest submerged. Nez was certain this Native American must be Atlantean. Standing upright, the time-traveler trudged up the hill and nodded at Nez.

Rocky climbed out of the pool and savored the bota bag's contents.

"What you fucking got there, man?" the biker that had been in the water asked.

"Plum wine," Rocky said, handing it to him.

The biker turned it upside down above his mouth, squeezed and puckered. "This stuff's too fucking sweet, man. Try this," pulling a pint bottle of Everclear from his jacket. Rocky raised it to his lips, sipped and winced.

"They put this stuff in dead people," he said, shaking his head, his body seconding the reaction.

"Fucking waste," the biker said, filling his cheeks with the stinging liquid and swallowing in one gulp.

Nez borrowed Virginia's camera. The bikers posed, taunting each other. The one who'd been in the pool didn't want to be photographed. He sat on a rock and watched the Indian. Nez followed the bikers up to the parking area, snapping away as they awakened their mechanical mustangs with a handlebar-grip twist and downward kick to the starter pedal, the two-wheeled beasts roaring to life.

"See you next fucking time, man," the biker that had been in the pool said as his girlfriend push-started them then climbed on and her boyfriend set the front wheel in the air. The other bikers waved and blasted down the two-lane to the highway, the growl of their engines fading and, except for Virginia's singing and the rustling of the leaves, the world becoming silent for one long moment.

"New Mexico really is the Land of Enchantment," Nez said to the sun, sky and mountains, talking to the terrain as clearly as it was speaking to him.

Virginia climbed out of the water. She and Rocky walked up the hill.

"Let's go into town for some lunch," Rocky said.

"I'll be right back." Nez walked down to the springs. The Indian was wrapping himself in a green blanket with white stars. As Nez focused the camera, his subject settled his arms at his sides.

"This is so people don't forget the Native Americans that lived here." Nez clicked.

As he turned to go, the Indian spoke: "The Spirit

Way is within you. It will reveal itself and lead you to your life's purpose."

Nez stopped and re-traced his steps. "For some time now I've had the feeling it would. Coming to New Mexico, meeting you and sharing this hot-springs day, I believe it will. Thank you. Good journey." Nez knew The Indian Man was an Ancient, like Virginia, timeless as Time. Making his way up to the road, he didn't look back, knowing if he did, the man would be gone. The only living that mattered was ahead.

Rocky drove. On the way to Santa Fe, the transcendental trio stopped in Las Vegas, New Mexico. Like Santa Fe, the town square was dressed for the Fourth of July. A mariachi band played in a whitewashed, half-round bandstand. Virginia translated the Spanish lyrics.

Each day is good. My love is here with me.
Every day will be the same as long as this is so.

They listened, transfixed. then walked across the square to the Don Quixote Lounge and sat at the table in the center of the room. A young waiter brought a bowl of chips and salsa. It was gone in minutes. The waiter came back with another bowl. Virginia ordered a salad with beans and rice. Nez couldn't decide and asked Rocky to order for him. Rocky ordered an enchilada for himself and a smothered burrito for Nez. Nez ate it in four bites.

"Nobody was going to steal that," Rocky said.

Nez caught the waiter's attention.

"Can we get a basket of bread?" The waiter nodded and went to the kitchen, but never brought the bread.

After lunch, Virginia read Nez's Animal Cards. Rabbit was his manifestation of Fear and Fox his Spirit Guide. Rabbit's Fear kept Nez from what he wanted. Fox traveled unseen, slinking at Nez's side, making Nez a ghost to most people, walking alone on his journey. Virginia offered to read Rocky's cards, but he declined.

"Knowing why I do things or why things happen takes the fun out of getting up every morning. I'll remain curious about what's going to knock me on my butt."

Out on the square, the mariachi band played. Burning mesquite scented the air. Rocky and Virginia savored their last bites of honeyed *sapopillas* (soh-puh-*pee*-uhs = *sofa pillows*, fried-dough fritters) as they walked to the car. Rocky took the wheel, Virginia rode shotgun and Nez sprawled on the back-seat.

Near Romeroville, Rocky said, "We've got to stop. I want to find my watch."

"Where'd it go?" Nez asked.

"I buried it around here somewhere seven or eight years ago."

Rocky inched the car to the shoulder of the highway.

Opening the rear passenger-door, Nez said, "Where do we begin?"

""It was on a rise and there was a big rock behind me."

"Lots of rises, lots of rocks," Nez said. "Why did you bury your watch, Sinbad?"

"I was hitchhiking and stopped in the forest to pray. I wanted to straighten out my life and I knew if I was asking for something I should give something in return, so I left the watch."

"You'll never be congressional material with that line of reasoning. How's your life now?"

"Still screwed up." Nez and Rocky howled.

"Well, hell," Nez said, wiping tears of laughter from his eyes, "let's at least get the damn watch back." Launching up the scrubby embankment and scuttling under a cattle-fence that hadn't seen a cow in some time, he entered a sparse, pine-desert forest, where he let his Indian-Man instinct lead.

There were more rocks to his left, so Nez trudged that way, following a short ridge, descending into an *arroyo* (uh-*roy*-yoh = a shallow, narrow valley) and scrambling up the far side overlooking a wide, green mesa with Santa Fe in the distance to the southwest. He picked up a stone and held it in his left hand, hoping to get a feel for his surroundings, and a clue as to which way to go. He could see Rocky and Virginia through the patchy trees to the north, walking the ridge. Then he spotted it: There it was, a large stone perched on top of an altar-like boulder with three small stones at its base. Nez removed them: ...one…two…three…no watch.

"This isn't the spot." It was Rocky. He and Virginia had crossed the arroyo in seconds when it should've taken them minutes. Nez figured Virginia had shape-shifted them to appear beside him through some time-compression technique she'd learned during one of her former incarnations.

"Looked like a good spot," Nez said.

"Let me ask my spirit guide." Virginia closed her eyes and held her arms out from her sides as she hummed what sounded like part chant, part incantation. Rocky and Nez watched in silence, then more silence.

"What's she saying?" Nez whispered.

"No idea."

Virginia lowered her arms and opened her eyes.

"What does your spirit guide say?" Nez asked.

"I got a busy signal."

Nez and Rocky roared, falling into one another and nearly to the ground. Nez picked up a Y-shaped stick.

"Let's divine for it." Holding the branch loosely in his hands, the Y pointing forward, and began to jerke up, down, left, right, then led them in a circle. "This isn't working," he said. "I'm not gettin' a good read."

"I think it's this way," Rocky said. Pointing up the ridge, he and Virginia trekked the way they'd come. Nez descended the arroyo, leaping and bounding down the steep rock face, following the creek bed a quarter mile then climbing up the other side. Walking in the opposite direction he'd gone the first time, he zig-zagged and came to some horses grazing.

"Horses, have you seen the rock where my partner buried his watch?"

The nearest paint shook its head and snorted.

"Thanks anyway."

Nez continued zig-zagging, getting less and less of a feel for where the watch was, and headed back to the Honda, no sign of Rocky or Virginia anywhere.

Nez opened the back door and stretched out on the seat, half in, half out of the car. Fifteen minutes later he sat up. Refreshed, he ate an apple, sprinkling each bite with an herbal lemon sauce he'd packed for the adventure. Retrieving a book from his bag, he read about the buffalo, staple of the American Plains Indian. Seventy-two million pounded the prairies until hunted by the white man to near-extinction in the 1850's. No animal in history had had a greater impact on any one civilization. The US government hoped the systematic killing of the buffalo would wipe out the Plains Indians. By 1901 there were only one hundred and eleven buffalo, and the government's plan had worked. President Theodore Roosevelt was wise enough not to let the buffalo disappear from the planet. Nez closed the book and tucked it in his sack.

Time passed, no watch and no Rocky or Virginia. Nez walked down the highway, calling for his friends and singing *Old MacDonald* as an *om* prayer then walked back to the car, stretched out like before and fell asleep.

"Honkster," Rocky said, opening the trunk. Nez sat up. It was late afternoon and had started to drizzle.

"Did you find it?" Nez asked, standing and stretching.

"No," Virginia said, "but we had a nice walk." She looked at Rocky and smiled.

"I don't think I'm supposed to find it," Rocky said. "Let's head back to the ranch."

"Yee-ha." Nez opened the driver's door. Winding the

Honda to fifty-five then seventy, they pulled in behind the Pink Adobe and swaggered arm-in-arm through Santa Fe's Old Town to the Ore House.

Two men were singing on the small stage of the second floor main room, one playing a *vihuela* (vee-*hall*-ah = mariachi guitar), the other, a guitarrón (gee-*tar*-rone = mariachi bass guitar). A group of inebriated tourists sang discordantly, swinging their arms and gulping beer between phrases as the three sun-drenched and rain-drizzled gringos entered. Rocky and Virginia plopped into a corner booth. Nez walked to the bar. Jersey was working. Her eyes met his.

"Howdy, dudester, what can I get you?" An inch taller than Nez, thin-boned and long-lined like an antelope, she had a lanky bounce to her step and curly, dark-brown, shoulder-length hair that smelled of jasmine.

"*Tres Coronas, Senorita*, and a shot of tequila big enough to stick my head in."

"Comin' atcha'." Jersey walked to the far end of the bar.

"A lovely sentiment," Nez said while she was still in ear-shot. Jersey flashed a smile over her shoulder.

Returning with the drinks, she said, "What did you do today?"

"We went to the hot springs at Hot Springs and

watched for a watch."

"Mmm." Jersey had no idea what Nez was talking about.

"You weren't at the dance hall last night."

"How do you know?"

"I went there, gangstered in, stood on a riser, cased the joint, didn't see anyone that looked like you, and thought, *That feline, rum-slider's playin' with my head*."

Jersey squealed.

"That's a good squeal ya' got there." Rocky had come to the bar.

"And it isn't even oiled up yet," she said.

"I'll get the oil," Nez said.

"Sounds like you gentlemen could use another shot. This one's on me."

"In that case, my partner would probably like to drink it out of your navel," Rocky said.

"Hold that thought," Jersey said, moving down the bar to serve a pair of flower-shirted tourists. She came back with the shots and the men drank them.

"You gentlemen enjoy this wonderful New Mexican evening," Jersey said, removing long-necked beer bottles from a case and placing them in the cooler behind her.

Rocky grabbed two beers and returned to the table. Nez picked up a wicker basket from a stack on a stainless steel cart and filled it with chips and salsa. The salsa was excellent, heavy on garlic. Nez stepped onto the porch. Two dogs were walking across the dark and relatively quiet square.

"Two dogs out walking...good idea for a song." He made his way through the barroom crowd, stopping briefly to listen to the mariachi players. then rejoined Rocky and Virginia at their table.

"How are you two doing?"

"I'm a whipped puppy," Virginia said, resting her head on Rocky's shoulder.

"Beat like a step-child," Rocky added, sliding his arm around her.

"I'll be right back." Heading to the bar, Nez thought another zap of tequila was what the declining evening required. Placing a shot glass on the bar in front of him, Jersey suspended the bottle's lip high above the glass's rim, both eying the space between. Then she tipped the bottle and let the golden liquid fill the shot-glass. Only one drop ended up on the bar.

Nez raised the elixir to his mouth like a cup of Communion wine and drank half in one gulp.

"Hoo-wee, girly-pie, that's what this barn dance needed. I'm going to hang with my associates a tad longer and perchance saunter hither anon. Stay cute, boot-scoot and boop–boop-ee-doop." Jersey winked, turning a towel around a beer mug, a wicked smirk on her face. Nez crossed the barroom.

"Who wants tequila?"

"None for me, Beezer," Rocky said.

"Mmm. I'll have a sip," Virginia purred.

Handing her the shot-glass, Nez laid down on the over-sized couch next to the table and tucked the bowl of chips and salsa under his chin. A waitress wearing a name-tag proclaiming her to be Melissa arrived.

"Would you like to see a beer list?"

"Surprise me with something Mexican in a bottle," Nez said, and felt a hand cradling his neck. It was Jersey placing a pillow with a Navajo spirit design under his head. "If I fall asleep and dream of you, it'll mean trouble for both of us," he cautioned, looking into her eyes.

"*That* kind of trouble doesn't scare me," she said, caressing his shoulder and returning to the bar in that flouncy stride Nez was enjoying more each time he was privileged to observe it. Closing his eyes, he sighed. The music played. The pungent garlic reminded him of his Italian grandfather. On the inside of his eye-lids his mind projected a long row of shoulder-high tomato plants in a tiered garden. His Uncle Berk's Beagle, Tina, was romping in and out of the rows. Nez remembered the day his uncle came home carrying her in a box.

"We were hunting. Two German Shepherds killed her. I couldn't get to her in time. She had no chance."

Standing next to the open door of Uncle Berk's Rambler, Nez held Tina's head in his hands. Looking down the hill at the river, he cried, imagining her soul floating on the water. He remembered thinking of her at the hot springs today and pondered how the subconscious pops re-occurring images into the mind.

His grandfather came out of the house. "These things happen." He was holding a withered basil plant.

They buried Tina in the garden along the fence between the tomatoes and grapevines. Nez could smell the sweet, tangy tomatoes and anise-scented grape-leaves wrapping around him like an Indian blanket.

He was looking down at himself, watching a boy standing next to his grandfather and uncle over the freshly packed soil of Tina's grave. His grandfather had a toothpick dangling from the corner of his mouth. Nez reached for the toothpick in the corner of *his* mouth *in* Santa Fe. He could feel his life circling 'round New Mexico, spiraling upwards to this singular point, reaching out to grasp what the Indian Man had promised.

Eyes closed, Nez saw his grandmother with her long, white hair. "Bettina," his grandfather called her. She was sitting in front of her boudoir mirror, combing her waist-length tresses. She'd never learned to read English. On Sundays, she and Nez would laugh at the pictures in the newspaper comics, imagining what the story was. Sitting on her lap, he thought she'd be with him forever.

He was alone with her in her hospital room when she passed, lying on her side facing the window, trying to comprehend her last light of day. She closed her eyes, then opened them, staring upward. They fluttered, closed, and slowly reopened, fixed on the eternal journey that she was undertaking.

Her image faded and was replaced by a garden filled with tomato plants and grapevines reaching to the sky, a beautiful, inlaid, ivory barrette on a night stand and a beagle playing in the yard of a big, white, house.

He saw two ambulance men carrying his grandfather, strapped to a metal stretcher, down the narrow stairs of his grandparents' house.

"Where are you going, grandpap?" Nez asked with a child's concern and vague suspicion he was about to lose something irreplaceable.

"To the cemetery," his grandfather said, looking at Nez, the words like a slap to Nez's face.

There in the Ore House, the spirits of his deceased relatives and all the animals he'd ever known hovered around him, telling him their journey was good. He encircled them in a golden triangle of light and one-by-one their images dissolved to where spirits go when they leave this place. He heard a familiar voice.

"Here's your beer, man." It was Rocky. "The waitress didn't want to disturb you."

"I finished your tequila," Virginia said.

Nez sat up. "It's a New Mexican Fourth of *Ju*-ly weekend." Standing, he headed to the bar. It was closing time and Jersey was cleaning up. "Do me for one more, cowgirl."

Jersey poured a double shot and lifted it to eye level between them. As Nez reached for it, she raised it to her lips, tossed it into her mouth and leaned across the bar. Nez knew what must come next.

Their lips met. The blast of igneous liquid passed from her mouth to his as cool as Mr. P. said it would, his heart doing a handstand like the Indian Man in the creek, the elixir bee-lining to his brain and making him think, *If I could drink starlight, it would taste like this woman's kisses.*

Jersey swung her legs over the bar and Nez swept her into his arms, swirling her in a Dionysian cowboy dance, dipping her and feeling the air go out of both of them. Raising her to meet his lips, they inhaled simultaneously and stood. It was as if life was beginning a new phase. Nez thought he could live in this one forever.

"He does that with all the waitresses he meets," Rocky said. He and Virginia were standing by the door.

"Let's do this again in the not-too-nebulous future," Nez said to Jersey, holding her around the waist. She squealed, hands on his shoulders.

Following his friends down the stairs and out onto Old Town Square, they walked like pilgrims on a holy land journey, singing Old MacDonald as an *om* prayer until they arrived at the Silent Indian Hotel. Virginia laid on the bed, pulling Rocky down next to her. Nez curled in the corner, wrapped in his Indian blanket, dreaming of the stark, high desert outside Madrid, he and Jersey spinning as one until they passed out dizzy with desire. The night wind was a voice and though he couldn't make out what it was saying, it was good news.

Virginia was sitting on Rocky's lap when Nez returned from the bathroom next morning, her slender legs extending from the hem of her red robe down to her red-painted toenails. Later, Rocky told Nez he'd washed her feet as the sun was coming up, a spontaneous, reverent gesture.

"You're becoming quite the metaphysically-metaphorical man."

"The things we do." Rocky said.

They sat on the floor, Virginia with her legs crossed in lotus position, Nez lying on his side, Rocky squatting, hands on his thighs to brace himself. Virginia was explaining the Soul Centers, how each generates a frequency in the color spectrum of the natural world and relates to a specific part of the human anatomy.

"The Soul hovers six inches above the Body, bathed in white light. The top of the head is the home of Higher Purpose, Mental Clarity, Transmutation of Negativity and Judgment. It corresponds to the color gold. Blue is the color of the brain, the home of Fear and Doubt. The throat is the center for Communication. Its color is green." Nez and Rocky listened like Buddhist monks at the feet of the Dalai Lama's easy chair. "The chest houses the Will and takes the color purple. The heart holds a ruby red light, the symbol of Love, Anger, Resentment, Healing and Forgiveness." Virginia talked about the Archangels and the Elements they correspond to. "Uriel is Earth; Michael, Fire; Gabriel is Water; Raphael, Air." Nez imagined them as restaurant Big Boys with cream pies ready to sling at anyone claiming *their* religion as the one true path.

It was noon when Virginia finished her hypnotic

monologue. She had to be leaving for Ojo Caliente where she'd be teaching the rest of the summer. They agreed to meet at five p.m. at the mineral springs in Ojo. Nez and Rocky loaded the Honda with knapsacks and guitars then wound their way on foot through Old Town, people-watching and peering in shop windows.

A boy selling newspapers held one up for preview. On the front page Nez and the General were shaking hands. The headline read, "Fourth of July Unites Diverse Cultures."

"The things we do," Rocky said and bought three copies. Nez took one and searched the back-page for *Robotman.*

"Does it have *Robotman*?" Rocky asked.

"No," Nez said, folding the newspaper and tucking it in his shorts at the crook of his back.

"Never trust a publication that doesn't print your favorite comic strip."

Skirting the square, they came to a red-brick art gallery with wide picture windows. Through the glare of the glass, making a sizable impression with his huge frame, puffed face and bulbous hands, Native American painter R. C. Gorman sat signing poster-prints of lazily transfixed Navajo women, baskets and pottery on their heads and at their sides. He was attended by two young women, one pale, waspish and urban, the other dark-skinned, exotic and feral, with long, thick, black curls framing her face. While R. C. autographed purchased prints and flashed his tight smile for each paying customer, Nez trained his gaze on the dark-complected attendant. Staring at him, she half-closed her eyes, tilted her head back and parted her generous lips, heaving her prodigious chest as if trying to catch her breath. Sensing something amiss, R. C. nudged her and looked out the window to see if Coyote or an evil curandero (coo-run-*dair*-oh = Mexican healer/folk doctor/shaman) was enchanting his assistant. Flustered, she put her free hand to her temple and rubbed it as if clearing her thoughts, then handed R.C. another print. Rocky noted the conjuring.

"Where'd you learn to do that, honkster?"

"Same place I learned to make women squeal, back of a cereal box. Let's go in."

Inside the gallery, they hovered at the wine and cheese table, partaking of snacks and fermented spirits, then proceeded to make an art stroll. In a back room, a petite, brown-eyed brunette in a tight, black dress and matching heels was talking up R. C. originals to someone on the phone. She spoke with her entire body, balancing her weight on one leg, one hand folded on top of the other with the phone tucked between her raised shoulder and left ear, proselytizing like a politician trying to get a bill passed fifteen minutes before Congressional recess. Her fingernails were the color of cantaloupes. Nez wondered if her toenails were the same color.

"I wonder if she paints her toe nails that color?" Rocky said. Nez noted the synchronicity—more Land of Enchantment magic.

In the main studio they moved like ghost dancers through the throng of art-patrons and tourists, slithering like lizards out the gallery door into the festive sunshine and bustle.

They walked next door into a ladie's shop, where the clerk inquired, "Can I help you?" She was tallish and slim with a Joan Rivers hairdo.

Nez was wondering if the sun, wine and New Mexico's alchemy were exerting their surrealistic effects on Rocky when he said, "We'd like to spend four hundred dollars apiece on our wives."

Nez was certain of two things, neither had a wife or four hundred dollars to spend. Rocky was playing Honskter, the object of the game being to get someone to believe a fabulous tale. If the person did, he or she'd been honskstered.

Nez did an about face, Rocky nearly falling over

him.

"What's this 'we' stuff? You have a mouse in your pocket?" No time for an answer.

Rocky said, "Show us your wares."

And your wherefores and whatnots, Nez thought.

The sales-clerk showed them everything in the store. Nez spotted a pair of leather pants with a flap in the back. "An emergency exit." The woman feigned a smile.

Nez wandered off while Rocky negotiated rack after rack. Tiring of the game he said, "Perhaps we should bring the little ladies in and let them pick and choose for themselves." The saleswoman's smile soured.

"Do you have a business card?" Nez asked politely.

"Yes," she replied curtly, realizing this wasn't going to be a big sale. "My name is Joan," she added with as much professional courtesy as possible.

"That was a devious piece of charlatanism," Nez said when they were on the sidewalk again. "I'm going to have to start calling you Honk Hogan." They were laughing as Nez noticed the marquis above a shop on the corner. "I'll be damned, a Woolworths."

"You'll be damned alright," Rocky said.

"All Woolworths smell like popcorn and chewing gum. Company policy," Nez said, pushing on the glass double-doors, leaving the modern-day-sidewalk crowd behind and entering a 1950's department-store world.

Worn into gentle troughs from years of people passing down the aisles, the pine-board floor moaned, announcing their presence. Nez made his way to a post-card rack and bought four, one of a rattlesnake, another of an Indian sand-painting, one of a cowboy sticking his head in a horse trough and a steam train blowing a long breath of black smoke.

"Pretty neat, don't you think?" Nez asked, fanning the cards in front of Rocky.

"Tried it once. Hurt so bad, I had to give it up."

"Buying cards?"

"Thinking."

Nez examined the beaded bracelets for sale, placing a dozen on each arm, topping them with a beaded hair-band. People stared. He looked in the mirror for several seconds then removed them all and headed for checkout. Rocky had two postcards, one of a neon cowgirl wearing heart-shaped sunglasses and waving over her shoulder from the driver's seat of a lime green Cadillac, the other, a lone cowboy on a horse leading a pack-mule down a steep, snowy mountain trail.

"Let's blow this popsicle-stand and visit my aunt and uncle," Rocky said.

"You've got relatives that admit it?"

Laughter carried them out the door, across the square and down Alameda past the Dragon Room Lounge to the Pink Adobe parking lot. Nez rummaged a bottle of Mad Dog Kiwi Lime from the backseat.

"Do you see a sign that says 'No drinking in this parking lot'?"

"Can't say I do," Rocky said.

"You drive."

They eased out of the parking lot and down a narrow, winding street past Loretto Chapel with its famous spiral staircase. No one knew the actual story, but the staircase was said to have been miraculously accomplished.

The most popular version was that a carpenter came to town looking for work in exchange for food. The church needed a staircase to the choir-loft. Wishing the carpenter well, the priest went missioning in the hills. Returning four days later, he was greeted by a magnificent, hand-carved, spiral staircase and no carpenter. The Sisters of Loretto say it was Jesus, but he didn't leave a business card or forwarding address.

"Let's go in," Nez said. Rocky parked the car.

The chapel was refreshingly chilly and candle-lit. Whispers echoed off the high, adobe walls. Behind the sacred staircase, away from the crowds, a Middle Eastern man knelt before a statue of the Virgin Mary. Finalizing his ritual, he stood and caught Nez staring.

"You looked intense," Nez said.

"I have traveled far to pray here."

"You were praying to the Virgin Mary?"

"I was praying *for* the Virgin Mary."

"She can use the kind words," Nez replied, staring up at the holy wooden corkscrew until the image burned in and faded out. When Nez's attention finally returned back to the room, the man was gone. Nez searched the entryway and outside the front door. The pilgrim was nowhere to be found. "First, the Carpenter," Nez voiced, shrugging "Now, this Muslim…"

"Let's go, honkster." It was Rocky walking past him out into the sun.

"Gotta' drink more or drink less," Nez said, quickstepping to catch up, "'cause the amount I'm drinking is giving me spooky visions."

Rocky maneuvered the Honda out of Old Town into a residential neighborhood. "It's around here someplace. This is the same wrong turn I made last time."

It was a low-key, Southwestern, middle-class neighborhood of wood, stone, stucco and adobe homes, most with xeriscaped lawns. Flat gravel or small-stone swatches highlighted patches of native plants and grasses.

Large, flat rocks lined the pathways like low-hanging mesas.

"I'd hate to have to mow one of these," Nez said.

Pulling to the curb in front of a one-story, beige-stucco ranch-style house with sky-blue window awnings, they ascended a sloping flagstone path to a carved oak door. Rocky knocked and ten seconds later his uncle greeted them—a Southwestern tan; thin, white, combed-back hair; what was once a muscular frame still showing in his arms and legs. Wearing black shoes, white socks, black shorts and a bolo tie pulled loosely over a powder-blue, short-sleeved, four-pocket, Mexican-rancher shirt, he was holding a yapping, white poodle sporting a blue bow on the crown of its head.

"Uncle, this is my friend, Nez."

"Nice to meet you, sir," Nez said.

"Come in," Rocky's uncle said. "I'm sitting out back in the garden. You fellas like a cold one?"

"Yes," was the double reply.

Rocky's uncle went into the kitchen and came out with two bottles of Modelo dark. Rocky told his uncle about Nez's musical abilities.

"What do you play?"

"Guitar, harmonica and mandolin." Rocky's uncle disappeared into the house and came out carrying two mandolin cases.

"I've had these a long time," he said, dusting them off and opening the larger one. "This is the 1952 Montgomery Ward I played in high school." It was tear-shaped and when Nez plucked its strings it broadcast a sufficient, even tone. Opening the second case, he said, "My grandmother played this one." It was a 1920's Martin musical treasure, red sunburst cedar with a pearl-inlayed fretboard. Missing one of its A-strings, it was still tuned true.

Strumming it, Nez said, "It's a wonderful instrument. Hums like the Universe."

"Have you heard of Dick Dia?" Rocky's uncle asked. Nez admitted he hadn't. "Dick Dia had a mandolin orchestra in the 50s and 60s." Uncle went inside and put a vinyl 78-LP on the phonograph turntable. Mandolin, mandocello and other mando sounds flowed from the sliding-glass entrance like belly dancers moving their bodies behind the floor-length curtains. Nez recognized the theme from *Never on Sunday*.

"I had a girlfriend who was crazy about that song," Nez said. "She moved to Vermont and married an architect."

Pleased to be part of their New Mexican adventure, Rocky's uncle said, "Come see my garden," indicating the way with a generous sweep of his arm.

Situated on a gentle hillside sprawling up two-thirds of the yard, the top of the hillock braced the neighbor's fence. They climbed and wandered beneath sweet-smelling piñon trees, talking about native plants and foreign species introduced to the area by explorers and settlers. Dick Dia's orchestra set the mood. Nez felt like Zorba the Greek.

"You can see all of Santa Fe from here," Rocky's uncle said when they reached the highest terrace. He'd dug an underground doghouse that curved into one far corner. "We had a Weimaraner. He liked to go in there and escape the heat. We had to put him down."

"Why is that?" Nez said.

"Liberal. Wanted to give the country away."

"Instead of selling it like a Radical Conservative?"

Rocky's uncle smiled. "Bad hips. He was only six."

"Uncle worked for the Forest Service," Rocky said.

"Yosemite and the Smoky Mountains," his uncle said. "It's good to be back in New Mexico."

"It's a great place to visit," Nez said.

"Would you gentleman like another beer?"

"No, thank you, Uncle," Rocky said. "We should be going. We need to be in Ojo Caliente by five."

"It's three now," his uncle said. "Here." He pulled

some plant bulbs out of the ground. "Take these Egyptian onions. Keep them moist and warm and they'll take off like you won't know what." Nez accepted the bulbs, trying to think of a phrase to fill the missing metaphor. After several seconds he was convinced *he didn't know what*.

"Thank you," he said.

At the front door, Rocky's uncle said, "Have a good adventure," lifting his beer in salute.

"From what we've experienced already, I believe this *is* the Land of Enchantment."

As the highwaymen walked the stone pathway to the car, Rocky's uncle said, "Your aunt will be sorry she missed you."

"Tell her I'm sorry I didn't get to see her."

"I will."

"Good-bye and thank you," Nez said, then to Rocky, "Full sail ahead, honkster."

Down the hill past the stone gardens they went like wisps of wind curling into the hills above Santa Fe. Neither knew how to get out of town going the right way.

Rocky made a u-turn into a liquor store parking lot. Two dark Mexicans in denim work clothes were dancing to Tejano music booming from the cab of a dusty, Datsun pick-up. A three-legged dog stood braced against the liquor store door-jamb, motionless except for a twinge in his one rear leg. He was staring Nez down like Indian Man at the hot springs.

"Friend of yours?" Rocky asked.

"We hopped a freight train once. He made a wrong step."

The dog winked slowly as if in agreement with the explanation.

"Hello, old dog. Good to see you again. I'll get you an ice cube while I'm inside," Nez said, walking past the mutt as it made a three-point, one-hundred-and-eighty-degree turn, spinning like a compass needle on its axis and leaned against the door-jamb facing into the store. Six feet inside, Nez stopped to survey the liquor store. Rocky skirted around him.

"You going to redecorate the place?"

"Neo-bowling alley," Nez said. "What do you think?"

"Tried it once. Hurt so bad, my head almost caved in." Rocky walked to the back of the store. The old dog skittered to the head of each aisle as Nez passed from one to the next. "That dog's following you," Rocky said.

"The wined leading the gimpy. We're going to enter a potato sack race, you know, each with one leg in the bag."

"You've already got one leg in the bag," Rocky said, "and your head's in there too. Take pictures."

"I won't, if you won't," Nez said. "Let's get some tequila, and Mad Dog if they have any."

"This is New Mexico. They *have to have* Mad Dog. It's mandated by state law."

"I'm going to hunt for some stout," Nez said, scratching the three-legged dog behind the ears and under the chin. "Hey, look, *Coyote* Tequila. That's a sure sign of something. Hmmm." He read the label. "Says here it's spiced with herbs. This is a must-try item." Rocky stepped to the counter.

"Do you have cold Mad Dog?"

"This is New Mexico," the clerk said. "It's mandated by state law. What flavor?"

"Kiwi Lime," Rocky said. The clerk reached into a cooler to his left and pulled out a bottle.

"Here you go."

"You keep the good stuff up front," Rocky said. "I love the fast, friendly service here. And a bag of ice." He paid. "Let's motor, honkster," he said, walking past Nez standing in the doorway petting the dog. Breaking the bag of ice into a garbage can lid, Rocky said, "Knock yourself out." The dog barked three times.

"Thank you," Nez said, "We certainly will." Nez

bounded down the stairs to the passenger side of the Honda.

"What did the Old Dog say?" Rocky asked.

"Have sweet adventures and don't let Coyote trick you again."

Rocky put the key in the car door and said to the dog, "Thanks, same to you." The dog stood at the top of the porch stairs wagging its tail and crunching ice cubes, watching the cosmic caballeros pull out of the parking lot.

"Did you get directions?" Nez said. Rocky put the car in reverse and backed to where the two Mexicans were dancing.

"How do we get to Ojo Caliente?" The dancers clung to one another breathlessly.

"Take this road to Española (Ess-span-nih*yol*a)," the señor said, "and go north out of town on it. At El Quende (*Qwen*-day) it becomes Highway 285. Take that all the way to Ojo Caliente." He was clutching a bottle of Mad Dog. Nez held his up. The Mexicans let out cackles that turned into singing, the dog bayed like a coyote through a mouthful of ice and Nez howled a belly-laugh of one-part mysticism and two parts madness, one part madness each for him and Rocky. The mysticism distributed itself across the New Mexican evening, calling them into its stark, high-desert adventure. Opening the Mad Dog, Nez tipped it to his lips as the Honda rolled out of town into the cool, redstone, New Mexican back-country west of Santa Fe, past Tesuque (Teh-*soo*-kee) Pueblo and Camel Rock.

"Looks like the camel on the cigarette pack," Rocky said.

"Now I know why I hang out with you."

They motored through Cuyamunge (Koo-yuh-*mun*-guh) to Pojoaque (Po-*walk*-ee), stopping at a Lotta' Burger hamburger stand. Rocky ordered Mexican and struck up a conversation with a young couple from Española (Ess-span-nih-*yo*-luh). Nez ordered American and walked to the floor-to-ceiling window, listening to Rocky and the couple. The young man was telling a joke.

"These tourists walk into this Lotta' Burger here in Pojoaque an' ask an old Indian sitting here how to pronounce the name of the place. In a solemn voice the old Indian says, 'Lotta' Burger'." The young man laughed, his girlfriend smiled meagerly, Rocky made an 'I *think* I got it' face and Nez made a mental note to try the joke on Virginia. They picked up their food and pioneered west to Española.

Mostly Mexican with Caucasians and Indians sprinkled in, for the entertainment of the people waiting at the interminably long light at one Española intersection, a Chevy low-rider station wagon filled with men, women, children and grandparents stopped, lowered, then raised its chassis, then lowered its front and back ends, then bounced its front tires. The other low-riders at the intersection honked approval.

Nez said, "I'll drink to that," and up-ended the Mad Dog.

Rocky said, "You'll drink to anything. If I lived here, I'd go into the shock absorber business."

"And I'd sell hydraulic fluid."

"What was left after you got done drinking it."

"I'm strictly a cleaning products man," Nez said, tipping the bottle again.

The light turned green. At the next one they missed the sign for Highway 285 and headed north-*east* out of town on Highway 68. They realized they were on the wrong road when they reached Embudo (Em-*boo*-doh), both the map and a green and white sign telling them so.

The road had climbed steadily. The Rio Grande was a silver ribbon meandering through the shallow-cut valley edged by tall, wispy grasses that bent in unison with each on-coming breeze. An outdoor café sat on the far side of the river, wooden picnic tables scattered from the parking lot at the crest of the hill down the sloping grade to the water's edge like the skeletal backbone of a dinosaur dead a million years. Rocky maneuvered the Honda across the one-lane, wooden bridge and brought it to rest between a silver-gray Mercedes Sport with a license plate that read 'Hot – 1' and a gold BMW with a vanity plate that said 'HIS GIRL.'

"Movie stars and Mafia women," Rocky said.

"Bring your chalks," Nez said. "You can draw a picture of the river. Let's ask directions and write 'em down this time and call Virginia and tell 'er we're going to be late."

"Tell 'er we're going to be drunk too," Rocky said. They were three and a half hours off schedule. Nez had been keeping track of how off-track they'd become, but had lost track of when he'd lost track of keeping track. Nez sat at the nearest picnic table.

"That table's reserved," a freckle-faced, curly-haired, chipmunk-toothed, redheaded waiter said.

"By whom?" Rocky asked.

"Don't know," the waiter replied.

"Why?" Nez said.

"Don't know that either."

"Thanks for straightening us out," Nez said, standing.

"I wouldn't want to get the daily specials from him,"

Rocky said, following Nez up the porch stairs. The rickety screen-door made a high-pitched, singing squeak.

Inside, life preservers and fish-nets adorned the walls, oars and orange flags topping off the atmosphere like a set from *Gilligan's Island*. A potent mixture of mosquito candles and Bug-Off scented the air.

The floor was concrete, the windows set low, six to each wall. Everyone in the café turned to watch the Southwestern road-adventurers enter. Nez detected an angle to the floor.

"Is this room tilting?"

"No, Picasso," the bartendress said. "It must be you."

Nez and Rocky stood in the middle of the throwback-to-a-hundred-year-old-dance-hall-saloon re-done in island-theme, looking and feeling like highway banditos.

"Do we need shirts?" Nez asked, eyeing a hand-written sign specifically requesting such. The *Madre de la Barra* snarled like a lioness protecting her brood.

"We've got young girls here."

Not missing a beat, Nez said, "We've got women waiting for us when we get where we're going, but thanks anyway."

"Whenever and wherever that will be," Rocky

added. "In the meantime, we'd like some of your spirited liquid."

Tall, broad-shouldered and muscular, the bartendress offered no physical or facial indication she was going to fulfill Rocky's request any time soon. Instead, she continued drying mugs, ordering them into military rows on the bar, eying the road-worn ruffians over the tops of her glasses. Nez took a humbler tone.

"We're not from around here. What's good to drink?"

Still drying, and with curtness in her tone, she said, "We make an ale, a stout, a porter, a lager and a jalapeño beer." Her face was strained, tired of repeating the litany for people "not from around here" and especially traveling trouble-makers.

"What flavor is jalapeño?" Rocky asked.

The bartendress stopped wiping and squinted, muscles tensing like a sumo wrestler about to take on two opponents at the same time. Cracking her knuckles, she seemed to be counting to ten or at least a good seven. At six, her eyes widened and she gave the two men a death-look like Sasquatch threatening to kill the person wanting to tell everybody the monster is real.

"We'll have two jelly-peenos. Heavy on the jelly," Nez said.

The bartendress poured mechanically.

"If it's not too much to ask, could you slide 'em down the bar like in Westerns?" Rocky said.

Walking to where the two men stood, she set the beers on the bar between them. "That'll be five bucks."

Rocky paid. "Charming place you have here. We're going to mosey down and enjoy the river." Tasting his beer, he looked at Nez and in his best Cary Grant imitation said, "Join me on the veranda, won't you, Miles?" Nez snatched his beer and followed Rocky out the door. Stepping off the porch, they passed the reserved table no one had come for.

There were two picnic tables close to the river, each with a broken leg. Rocky placed a stone under the short side of one, pulled out his chalks and began drawing on the tabletop. Nez patrolled the shoreline where the river cut into the hillside, exposing a tangle of claw-like tree roots. A full, cream-colored moon was rising over the hilltop café, embossing the scenery in liquid silver.

"We should be going," Nez said.

Rocky slipped his chalks into his pocket and walked up to the parking lot. There, a beaten-up public phone hung crucified on a telephone pole. Nez hadn't seen one of those in a longer time than he'd seen a woman in a sequin dress. He phoned his parents. His mother answered and told him to get a good job with benefits. Nez tried to think of a good-paying job he might like and couldn't, but agreed to anyway. Rocky signaled for Nez to accompany him to a teepee across from the café.

They hunched and stepped in. The last rays of sunlight gave the air inside a yellow tint. Nez sat on the ground and Rocky on a folding lawn-chair, the only sound the irritated buzzing of a fly that had an important picnic to attend and couldn't find the door-flap. The chair reminded Nez of swimming with his cousins at his Aunt Lila and Uncle Jazz's years ago. His mother was filming in Super 8 and the films played back too fast, making everyone move Keystone-Kop fashion, the adults sitting on lawn chairs like this one in the teepee. It was a time when Nez believed the world was becoming a better place and he'd swim like that forever.

"Did you call Virginia?" Rocky said.

"Let's do it now."

Rocky drove south to San Juan Pueblo then west to Highway 285, the 'right' way to Ojo Caliente. The road climbed, peaking above a wide valley sprawling to the east. The last rays of sun burned a gold and orange-blue hole through the distant mountains. The moon watched the sun's demise as if to say, "It's my turn, now." Rocky stopped the car before the grand vista.

"Let's write that song."

"Which one?"

"*Desert Train*," Rocky said.

They pulled their guitars out. A motor-home raced down the hill like an errant meteor. The driver honked. Kids waved from every window.

"How's this for an opener?" Rocky said, singing,

"*Take the Desert Train down to Santa Fe.*"

"Not bad," Nez said. "And this:

Meet me in the square,
We'll go dancing there and fall in love."

"I like that," Rocky said.

The sun planted a big, wet good-night kiss on the valley below and the moon mopped it up to save for dew-drops next morning.

Satisfied with their musical and travel progress, Rocky and Nez loaded the car and the night swallowed them whole, spitting them out in Ojo Caliente, New Mexico —Population 21. A faded, green and white road sign announced that information. Slowing as they passed an abandoned hotel and café, Rocky waved down an

Indian in a pickup truck coming from where they were headed.

The Springs was, "Back there, on the right."

Rocky u-turned. Coming down the two-lane past the hotel and café through the darkness, he spotted Virginia's Peugeot. Flashing the Honda's high beams twice, the two cars nuzzled next to one another like porpoises comparing findings on whether global warming was real or something Al Gore had made up.

"For a guy who doesn't see in the dark too well, you know your Texas-Princess's headlights pretty well."

"Nice to see you, gentleman," Virginia said sweetly. "You're late, but who's keeping track of time in these high-desert nights?" With dark-eyed sparkle, she squealed like a grown-up pixie, full of New Mexican enchantment and mid-summer night dreams. "Follow me. We're going dancing in the temple."

"Worse things could happen," Rocky said.

"We shudder to think," Nez added.

Rocky u-turned one more time, shadowing the Peugeot past the deserted hotel and café like two dogs out walking.

Double déjà vu, Nez thought.

Coming to a washboard rutted road on the right, they turned up the hill. Driving mostly on the left side where it wasn't so gullied, the long dirt driveway leveled and widened, presenting two hogan-shaped buildings of identical size, each fifty feet in diameter with eight-foot, vaulted roofs. The Honda and Peugeot nuzzled next to the buildings like puppies suckling their mother, cutting their lights and engines like those puppies drifting to satisfied dreams.

Light streaming from the windows of the first building and the doorway of the second lit the parking area and added their light to that of the full moon to make the trio's arrival a brilliant affair. Nez grabbed the tequila and Virginia led them into the second building.

Inside the entryway, two dark-skinned women in peasant dresses and a Mexican-American male in jeans, white t-shirt and brown cowboy boots talked and sampled drum rhythms. The man introduced himself as an Albuquerque policeman. Nez thought it strange to meet a person who could police and drum, like something from a Tony Hillerman novel or just more New Mexican enchantment.

Placing the bottle of tequila on the floor next to a large bowl of fruit by the door to the main room, Nez stepped in.

The floor was plush-carpeted in a demure patchwork design. The room's windows were spaced every six feet, reminding Nez of the Embudo bar they'd been in earlier and the duck-hunting cabin he'd inhabited for two months one summer at the end of a sand road on Cape Cod. In the center of the hogan a three-foot stonework column supported a mature and mighty buffalo skull, its hollowed eyes and spiny nose-bridge accentuated in a grimaced, time-worn face. Like New Mexico's terra firma, the skull spoke in a wordless language that propelled Nez to the past and the future at the same time. Opening himself to its message, his shoulders and knees relaxed and his breathing became deeper. Closing his eyes and straightening his back, he inhaled the room's sage incense, recalling his Indian–dancer past-life, the drums like bees buzzing on a night a thousand years ago.

Virginia was using fluid, arcing arm movements as she spoke with a dark-eyed, olive-skinned woman dressed in a flowered, wrap-around sari with delicate bell chains on her ankles and dreadlocked hair veiled by a lizard-skin-patterned scarf. Tracing circles with her hands, Virginia's dark eyes glowed in the dim light. In response to Virginia's words, the woman stabbed the air with fierce joy, stepping side-to-side as she spoke.

The corner opposite the door was piled with drums and assorted rhythm instruments, some Nez didn't recognize. One was an engraved, wooden stick three feet long with a bear's head carved at one end. It had bells running its length and reminded him of the bear claw cloud he and Rocky had seen yesterday. A lanky man in his mid-twenties with long, brown hair and a short, neatly-trimmed beard approached

"Welcome to Hummingbird. My name's Todd," he said, offering his open hand.

"I'm Nez. This is a good place to come to." Nez pointed to the far corner where an organic altar had been set up. Based on the many offerings, it appeared to be utilized frequently. In a tiered portal was a statue of a shrouded woman like the Virgin Mary. Beneath her was everything from incense and flowers to a comic book and a Banana Moon Pie.

"Who does she represent?" Nez asked.

"Our Lady of the Well," Todd answered. In the dim light, she looked like a hand-carved maiden spotted in serene candlelight. Nez thought of the church staircase. It was his turn to be the praying Muslim.

There was jewelry and currency from around the world laid as offerings as well as prayer beads, books, scraps of paper with blessings, poems, words of wisdom, postcards, a pack of dominoes, a deck of cards with the aces sticking out the top, red and black licorice, a Tarot deck, a pair of dice showing Snake Eyes and a jar of water with a carved wooden cup. There were pieces of Christmas wrapping paper, several small birds' eggs, some chocolate eggs and a broken watch that reminded Nez of Rocky's out there somewhere near Romeroville.

There were photographs of families, young men in military dress, smiling women, bow-legged old men with their hands in their bib overalls, children standing in front of a church, a baby being bathed, a boy riding a pony and a little girl giving her daddy a kiss. A string of Christmas lights encircled the shrine.

Nez knelt and all sounds ceased, all movement stopped. From within the silence and stillness voices from another world spoke, like the time he looked into an aboriginal ceremonial dish and the tribesmen of New Guinea called him to hunt and celebrate their good fortune. Aged souls whispered prayers, mantras, incantations. Their messages ran through him at light speed, telling him to let Fear pass out of him through his feet to Mother Earth as fast as lightning reaches up from the earth and strikes the sky. Taking off the bandana around his wrist, he placed his tuning pipe and a guitar pic in it, folded the cloth and laid it on the altar between the wooden cup and the Moon Pie, looking up at Our Lady smiling down at him. Her pursed lips seemed to be humming.

"Gotta' dance," Nez said, rising from his knees, folding his hands to his forehead in prayer and bowing deeply. Whirling to face the dancers, he bounded across Our Lady of the Well's universe in a cosmic hop-scotch game, past the buffalo skull to the circle of drummers laying down a beat for the dancers to stitch a foot-pattern to, weaving the sounds into a living, pulsating astral quilt.

Rocky and Virginia stood at the edge of the circle, swaying to the beat. Nez matched his movements to the other dancers. Twirling ecstatically, he closed his eyes, the music painting his spirit a brilliant red.

Clasping the Bear Stick, Nez held it at chest height, shook it to the beat and was transported from this magical New Mexican hilltop. Geronimo came to him on horseback. Nez danced, shaking the rhythm stick, feeling it fill his body, one buffalo running, Geronimo fighting a tide too strong to quell. The music pounded to a halt.

"I thought I was in Belize, the way you played that stick," the policeman-drummer said.

"I was traveling without luggage, that's for sure."

The drummers began another rhythm. Nez walked to the archway, retrieved the tequila and wandered outside. In the light from the doorway, he noticed a puppy crouching at the near corner of the other building.

"Good evening, pup-pup. You live around here?"

The little dog took off running, disappearing between the two structures. A beat-up Nissan pickup and a banged-up Chevy Bel Air were parked out front. An antler rack hung above the door.

Nez maneuvered to the long side of the building and peeked in a window. Two men were playing darts and drinking beer. Through the glass he heard a Rolling Stones song playing.

Every town has a bar, Nez thought, *even one with a population of only twenty-one*. Moving back from the window and walking to the door, he pushed it open, stepping through the entryway into the large room. The man throwing darts stopped mid-swing. Sitting on a long work table and playing with a white kitten, the other didn't notice. Nez realized he was in a woodcrafter's workshop.

Over the Stones, Nez said, "Excuse me. I thought this was a bar. I heard the music and saw you guys playing darts from outside." The man sitting at the table looked up, but didn't say anything. "I've got a bottle of tequila," Nez said, holding it up. "May I offer you some?" Both men came alive.

"I'm Nez, from Denver."

"Kirby," the dart player said.

"Bob," the cat-handler added.

"Tequila?" Nez said.

"Almost killed me a couple times." Bob eased the kitten to the table and took the bottle. "'Used to love this stuff." He swallowed. "It'll make you crazy."

"That's why we drink it," Nez said. "Besides, *this* stuff is fortified with natural herbs and spices." Bob looked at the label then handed the bottle to Nez. Nez set it on the table.

Kirby picked it up and held it to the light.

"It's sorta' green." He tilted it to his lips. "Sweet too. Sweetest tequila I ever drank."

"I've got some Mad Dog in the car. We can use it for a chaser." Nez walked out into the darkness. In the moonlight, Rocky was pulling his guitar from the Honda's trunk.

"I'm gonna' play awhile."

"C'mon next door when you're done. I found the town bar." Nez scavenged the Mad Dog from under the passenger front seat. Crossing the gravel lot, he met the puppy, the kitten and an old, black dog making a huffing sound at the wood shop door.

"Let's go in and join the party," Nez said. The puppy pawed at Nez's thighs, the kitten bounded over the low garden fence into the darkness and the old, black dog walked to Nez's side.

"Happy hunting," Nez said in the kitten's direction. The dogs followed Nez in.

"I found your other dog," Nez said.

"Mad Dog," Bob said, shifting his weight and taking the bottle. Twisting the cap, he stuck his nose in the bottle's snout. "Smells like the stuff they put in dead people."

"That would be a waste of good, cheap wine," Nez said. Bob took a swallow.

"Tastes like medicine."

"That's because it is," Nez said. Bob plunked the bottle down on the table. Kirby picked it up. Rocky materialized in the doorway.

"Who took the cork off lunch?" Nez did introductions.

"This is Rocky. Rocky, this is Kirby and Bob." The old, black dog made a half-hearted growl. Kirby offered the Mad Dog to Rocky.

"Here's lookin' atcha' and screaming in terror," Rocky said, swallowing, wincing, and noticing the carved furniture about the workshop. Some of the pieces were large and impressive. "Nice stuff. What is this humongous thing?"

"An entertainment center for a doctor in Taos,"

Kirby said. "Your T.V. goes here, your audio stuff here and here." Kirby squatted and slid out a panel in the back near the bottom. "Here's where you stash stuff you don't want anyone to find." Kirby reached in, pulled out a joint, lit it and handed it to Rocky.

"Thanks for showing us that," Nez said. "Will you have to kill us now?"

Rocky said, "I'll be outside, gentlemen, and I use that term loosely."

"Gentlemen?" Bob asked.

Over his shoulder Rocky said, "Outside," disappearing into the darkness.

Kirby and Bob returned to their dart game. Nez looked at postcards tacked on a cork board by the door. The puppy and dog relieved themselves in a sawdust pile in the corner. The Mad Dog went around.

"Who's the woman with her shirt off taking a picture of whoever's taking a picture of her?" Nez asked, inspecting a photo tacked on the wall next to the postcards. He was about to compliment her sensuality when Kirby answered, "My ex." The Stones finished. The sound of a lone guitar oozed in through the open door. Bob turned to listen.

"What's that?"

"Rocky," Nez said.

"He's got a guitar?" Kirby asked.

"He's not making those sounds with his armpits," Nez said. "Come on." Like a cosmic Three Stooges they trudged into the northern New Mexican night, the dog and puppy following.

The moon was in full bloom. A few stars shone in an immense black-velvet sky. The air felt cool. Navigating towards the Honda, Rocky was sitting on the lip of the trunk, strumming. The drumming inside Hummingbird had stopped.

"Let's play," Nez said, pulling his guitar from the trunk. The Twisters launched into their set. Todd came out of Hummingbird with a drum. Kirby and Bob hooted and hollered at appropriate and inappropriate times.

Kirby downed the last zap of Mad Dog as Nez and Rocky finished their final song. Everyone howled. The kitten had come to the edge of the gathering, but fled for the safety of the garden when she heard the men baying like wild dogs.

The party ended, and Bob excused himself. He was in charge of the three a.m. feeding of their two-month old girl.

Kirby said, "Goodnight," and headed for his hammock slung between the buildings. The old black dog and puppy followed like soldiers.

"You guys can sleep in the temple if you like," Todd said. "Bring your guitars if you want to play awhile."

Inside Hummingbird, to the left of the main room, were Todd's living-quarters, decorated in neo-voodoo. Christ icons and other deities were scattered among clumps of drying plants draped over strings zig-zagging across the room. The walls and ceiling were covered with tapestried embroideries. Todd lit a match and held it to a candle on the table.

"My kinda' place," Nez said. "All it needs is a fire escape." He went out to find Rocky standing in the doorway, staring into the night.

"You okay?"

"Collecting my thoughts."

"I get my cleaning lady to do that. You want a paper bag or something?"

"I'll use my hat."

Nez went in and sat across from Todd.

"I'm making tea. You want some?" Todd asked.

Rocky came in.

"Let's work on *Desert Train*," he said.

"What's that?" Todd asked.

"A song about our New Mexican adventure," Rocky told him.

"What have you got so far?"

Rocky strummed and sang,

> "*Take the Desert Train*
> *Down to Santa Fe.*"

Nez harmonized.

> "*Meet me in the square.*
> *We'll go dancing there and fall in love.*"

"What it needs is another line to wrap up the thought," Rocky said.

"How's this?" Nez said.

> "*Don't leave me howling at the moon,*
> *I'm not looking for Coyote Love.*"

"I like it," Rocky said.

"Me too," Todd agreed, "and I have to throw you guys out. I didn't realize it's four-thirty. I have to be up at nine. Virginia has a seminar in the temple at ten."

Rocky said, "We'll be up by nine."

"Looking and smelling our best," Nez added, standing up and carrying their guitars into the main room.

Rocky exhaled. "It's great to be alive."

"But not awake," Nez said.

Rocky settled on the far side of the buffalo skull. A minute later he was snoring like a mystery train.

Nez opened the two windows nearest Our Lady of the Well, took off his clothes and wrapped himself in his Blue Star Blanket. Thinking about Geronimo and Lena and her kittens, he fell asleep, his spirit wandering the San Juan Valley, looking for an open window to fly in and a sleeping girl to kiss.

Nine a.m.

Rocky was up and gone. Nez heated the tea and walked outside. It was already hot. Lizards sunning themselves on the woodpile scattered as Nez approached.

Crossing the grass and gravel between the two hogans, Nez sat under the tree in front of Kirby's woodshop. Todd came out and rolled a cigarette. Rocky came up the hill with Virginia, his guitar slung across his back. Swinging it into position, he said, "Let's hammer out a second verse."

"You play and I'll moan along."

"I was thinking," Rocky said.

"Run for cover."

Rocky strummed the chords and Nez sang.

"*Spend another day,*

Ojo Caliente.
See the sun go down,
Darkness all around and stars above."

"I can live with that," Rocky said. "Okay, third line."

Nez continued,

"*Big moon hanging in the sky,*
You're the reason why Coyote howls."

"If I didn't know better, I'd say we were geniuses," Rocky said.

"Outstanding in our field, a lower forty of corn," Nez said. Todd nodded.

"Time to clean up and hit the road, honkster." Rocky stood and dusted himself off. Cars and people were arriving for Virginia's Past Life Reformation workshop. Rocky and Nez loaded the Honda and walked down the hill to Virginia's cabin. Rocky showered, then Nez reluctantly agreed to be rained on again. When he came out, Rocky was sitting on the bed playing *Desert Train*.

"Let's bang out a third part and take it all home," he said.

"Play it again, Spam."

Rocky strummed and they sang. When they came to the third verse, Nez said, "Here it is:

> *Moonlight on the rails,*
> *Shadows haunt the hills."*

"Aah, and this," Rocky said, adding,

> "*We'll go hand in hand*
> *Through this Enchanted Land,"*

and they knew the next words,

> "*New Mexico*."

They were Riders on the New Desert Train.

"Pretty nifty," Nez said.

"I'd drink to that, but it's too early," Rocky said. "I'll brush my teeth to it instead." Mouthful of toothpaste, he said, "We'll get the last line before we're in Denver," and spat in the sink.

They left the coolness and comforts of Virginia's cabin and walked up to Hummingbird. Kirby was unloading his pickup. His puppy was jumping up and down like it wanted to help. The three men exchanged good mornings and Rocky walked into the temple. Nez sat under the tree. Todd came out.

"More tea?"

"Don't mind if I do."

Todd went in and returned with a steaming mug, the state symbol of New Mexico emblazoned on it, a red sun with four rays blazing in each direction on a square yellow background.

"Thank you," Nez said.

Todd sat and rolled another cigarette. People were drifting out of the temple. Rocky and Virginia appeared. Several seminarians walked to the edge of the bluff and tossed rose petals, their offerings floating like red snowdrops over the abandoned motel and coffee shop. Eyes closed, arms outstretched, palms up, one man stood at the edge of the rise.

"Whatever he's releasing, I hope it gets good and gone," Nez said mimicking the seminarian's ritual. Opening his eyes and lowering his arms, he breathed deeply. "Life's good and gettin' better."

"We're making it up as we go," Rocky said. He and Virginia were behind Nez. Nez turned to face them. "Thanks for the adventure, Princess." He knelt to touch her feet. She squealed and Heaven ran to hear her.

"He's got a knack for making women do that," Rocky said, then added, "In the name of the Father, Son and Wholly Squealy."

"Aye, men," Nez said.

The trio walked to the waiting Honda.

"Take care, Todd," Rocky said. "See you around here sometime again," then to Nez, "Saddle up."

"Thanks for the night in the temple," Nez said to Todd. Kirby came out of his workshop with his dogs. The kitten poked its head from the garden. "Goodbye, animals. Keep carving, Kirby. Say good-bye to Bob. We're makin' like a bakery truck and haulin' buns."

Rocky and Nez climbed into the Honda, waved and headed to the highway, North on 285 through Carson National Forest, past Piedra (Pee-*ay*-druh) towards the Colorado state line.

"This's been more fun than I can't remember," Nez said, yawning. "Let's do it again sometime in the not-too-nebulous future."

Conejos (Koh-*nay*-yose) zoomed by. Alamosa dissolved in their dust. It started to rain. Mist shrouded the San Juan Mountains like sulking children despondent at the thought of having to play indoors.

Rocky pulled into a truck stop, and ordered the chicken-fried steak. Nez had a Caesar salad with a side of dry toast. The waitress forgot his toast and Nez didn't remind her.

It was pouring when they got back on the road headed for Walsenburg and the Interstate 25 hook-up that would take them back to Denver. When the rain stopped, Rocky steered to the side of the road. In the distance, a coyote watched from a hillock.

"Let's get that last line," Rocky said. Standing in the sunshine with one cowboy boot on the front bumper, Rocky played the song through. When it came to the end, Nez crooned,

> "*And Coyote on the hill*
> *Watches 'til that Desert Train is gone.*"

"Sings about right," Rocky said.

The camper filled with kids they'd seen on the way up to Ojo came down the hill, kids waving from the windows.

"Déjà vu," Nez said. "Wake me when you're driving off the road." Nez closed his eyes and rested his head on the window sill. Rocky commandeered the Honda up and over La Veta Pass.

Nez never did get his toasts and breads that weekend.

Scott Mastro

Blood Money

About the Author

Scott Mastro has lived all over the place and continues to do so. *Sticks & Stone ~ How the West Was Wonderful*, the first novel in the *Sticks & Stones* satirical-adventure series, will be published later this year, in which Dylan Sticks and Seamus Stones are living decrepit Dublin lives, until they steal a leprechaun's gold, inciting the wrath of a dragon, Scotland Yard, Barbary pirates, three warring American Indian nations and the biggest buffalo herd west of the Mississippi. Tom Sawyer, Huckleberry Finn, look out. *Sticks & Stones* are in town. A Readers Guide for *Blood Money ~ Tales from Two Continents* is available by emailing mastromuse@gmail.com.

If you enjoyed *Blood Money,* consider these other fine books from Savant Books and Publications:

A Whale's Tale by Daniel S. Janik
Tropic of California by R. Page Kaufman
Tropic of California (the companion music CD) by R. Page Kaufman
The Village Curtain by Tony Tame
Dare to Love in Oz by William Maltese
The Interzone by Tatsuyuki Kobayashi
Today I Am a Man by Larry Rodness
The Bahrain Conspiracy by Bentley Gates
Called Home by Gloria Schumann
Kanaka Blues by Mike Farris
First Breath edited by Z. M. Oliver
Poor Rich by Jean Blasiar
The Jumper Chronicles by W. C. Peever
William Maltese's Flicker by William Maltese
My Unborn Child by Orest Stocco
Last Song of the Whales by Four Arrows
Perilous Panacea by Ronald Klueh
Falling but Fulfilled by Zachary M. Oliver
Mythical Voyage by Robin Ymer
Hello, Norma Jean by Sue Dolleris
Richer by Jean Blasiar
Manifest Intent by Mike Farris
Charlie No Face by David B. Seaburn
Number One Bestseller by Brian Morley
My Two Wives and Three Husbands by S. Stanley Gordon
In Dire Straits by Jim Currie
Wretched Land by Mila Komarnisky
Chan Kim by Ilan Herman
Who's Killing All the Lawyers? by A. G. Hayes
Ammon's Horn by G. Amati
Wavelengths edited by Zachary M. Oliver

Scott Mastro

Almost Paradise by Laurie Hanan
Communion by Jean Blasiar and Jonathan Marcantoni
The Oil Man by Leon Puissegur
Random Views of Asia from the Mid-Pacific by William E. Sharp Jr.
The Isla Vista Crucible by Reilly Ridgell

Soon to be Released:

In the Himalayan Nights by Anoop Chandola
Perverse by Larry Rodness
On My Behalf by Helen Doan
Rules of Privilege by Mike Farris
Light Surfer by David Allan Williams

http://www.savantbooksandpublications.com